CRANE HOCKEY

# ONE
## *pucking*
# HEART

USA TODAY BESTSELLING AUTHOR
## ELLIE WADE

*This book is dedicated to Suzanne Talkington
my hockey romance-loving friend.
Thank you for all your love and support
over the years. So grateful for you.
And, sorry about your team's loss…
it just had to be ;-)*

# CHAPTER
## ONE

BECKETT

*W*ell, this fucking sucks.

The moment that asshole in his yellow-and-black jersey comes barreling into me, smashing me into the boards, I feel it. The twist of my body, the unnatural angle of my leg as I'm slammed between the one hard surface and a hotheaded dipshit. I'm all for a good fight during a hockey game, but this was uncalled for. It's not a fight but an attack.

I never aim to hurt another player, even when I despise them. Would I enjoy giving a deserving opponent a black eye or busted lip? Sure. Who wouldn't? But I'd never want to cause them irreparable harm. It's a mutual respect. As deep as rivals go, the fact is we all love this game. We wouldn't be here if we didn't. This game is our life, our livelihood, our stress relief, and, in my case—my family. It's everything to me, and as I fall to the ice, I'm terrified I've lost it.

I'm no stranger to injuries. I've broken or sprained so many parts of my body playing this game over the past twenty years that I've lost count of them all. When I was a child, the emergency room staff at our local hospital called me a frequent flier. My mother would take me in, and the nurses would look at her in question as if to say "your kid is hurt again?" My mom would utter one simple word—hockey—and the nurses would nod knowingly.

This game has been the most important thing in my life since I was six years old. Hell, I'm quite sure I subconsciously chose my best friend because I knew he'd be great at the sport, and I needed someone to practice with. The idea of something taking me out early is my worst nightmare. Maybe that's dramatic, but it's the way it is. This is more than a game to me. It's everything.

So, yeah... this injury feels different. Everything is off, from the position of my body when I'm hit to the way I fall to the ice to the sheer pain radiating up my leg. I catch my best friend Cade's stare as I hit the ice, and I can see the state of my injury reflected back at me. It must look as awful as it feels because Cade takes one look at me, and rage consumes his features.

He flies toward my attacker and throws his gloves off, pounding on the jerk's face. With a flurry of movement, Sebastian Calloway, our center, joins the fight.

I try to push my body from the ice but can't move my leg. Our hometown fans go crazy in the stands, the sound deafening, and I hate that they have to see me this way. I equally despise that my parents and sister, who are somewhere in the crowd of navy-and-white jerseys, have to witness this.

The team medics are at my side, giving me instructions, but my focus is across the ice as Bash and Cade are escorted to the penalty box, along with the douche, Kyle Whitmore, from Pittsburgh. The medics help me up onto my good leg, and I take in the time on the clock—less than five minutes left.

Our NHL team from Michigan, the Cranes, has had an amazing run this year. Cade and I were drafted to the Cranes right out of college. This is our fourth year here, and in that time, this is the best our team has been collectively. We have the right combination of talent, personalities, and that something special that makes a team great. This was supposed to be our year. We were first in our division and entered the Stanley Cup playoffs in round one against the team from Pittsburgh. We should've beat them and moved on by the fourth game. Yet here we are in game seven in a three-game tie. The winner of this game will move on to round two of the playoffs.

The score is currently one to one. A goal would seal the deal for either team, and half of our guys are off the ice. Bash and Cade will be in that penalty box for the rest of the game, and I'll be on my way to the hospital. It will take a miracle to pull out a win, and somehow, I just don't see one coming.

The game resumes while I'm put on a stretcher off the ice and rolled out of the arena, where I'm lifted into an ambulance. The sight of my mom running toward the ambulance in my number eighteen jersey causes the dam that's been holding my emotions in to break.

Bitter, angry tears fall.

"Wait, I'm his mom," she shouts, climbing into the ambulance. "I'm coming with him."

She doesn't wait for permission because nothing would keep her away. She's always been my most fierce protector and a wonderful mother.

My chest heaves as tears roll down my face. A mix of anger, regret, fear, and sadness consumes me. "Mom," I choke out as she takes my hand.

She gives me a warm smile. "It's okay, my love. It will be okay. I promise."

"It feels different," I state.

I've heard many stories of catastrophic knee injuries taking players out for good, and the amount of fear bubbling beneath the surface over this possibility is more than I can handle.

"Listen." She runs her fingers through my hair, moving it away from my face like she did when I was a little boy. "We aren't going to worry until we talk to a doctor, okay? Think positive."

I nod.

"Dad is following in the car, and Iris will head over with Cade." She rubs her thumb against the skin of my hand.

With a dip of my chin, I acknowledge her again.

The hospital was prepared for my arrival, and the staff wastes no time. My uniform pants are cut from my leg, and I'm put into a bulky plastic brace before I'm wheeled off to the radiology department, where I get an MRI.

After the scan, I'm taken to a patient room, where my parents wait. It's rare to see my dad in a hospital room. Hell, it's rare to see my dad, period. He's a hotshot lawyer with his own firm and is somewhat of a workaholic. Having him at my game tonight was an unusual event. Regardless, it's nice that he's here.

My mom rushes to my side. The nurse, all five feet of her, locks the bed in place and tells us that the doctor will be in to update us soon. She's a tiny woman —young and attractive enough. She lingers in the room longer than is needed and retakes the measurements of my leg for my brace three separate times. She checks my vitals more than once and fiddles with a machine on a pole not even connected to me. She instructs me on how to use the TV remote and call button if I need anything, all while gifting me with a lingering smile and stolen touches. I assure her I'm fine.

I'm not oblivious to the flirting. Not to sound like an arrogant ass, but I'm used to it. Let's be honest, I lucked out in the looks department, have a kick-ass personality, and make millions playing a professional sport. Of course she's doting on me and providing special attention. Normally, I'd be all about it. Hell, I've had more one-night stands than I can remember. But at this moment, I just want her to leave. My career may very well be over, and that devastation outweighs a booty call any day.

My mother clears her throat and pins the nurse with a stare. "We're good. Thank you so much." Her tone is sweet as can be, but the message is clear. *Leave.*

The nurse blinks, and with a shy smile, she exits the room.

With a shake of her head, my mom releases a breathy laugh. "What is it with you and women?"

"I can't help if I'm a catch, Mom." I raise my shoulders with a forced smile, trying to keep the air light.

My father grumbles something from his chair in the

corner of the room, but I don't attempt to decipher it. I have enough on my plate without his judgments.

The door swings open, and my sister, Iris, rushes in. "What did they say?" Her eyes are wide as she looks from me to our mother.

"No word yet," Mom answers. "He had an MRI, and we're waiting for the doctor to read it."

She blows out a breath. "Okay."

"Where's Cade?" I ask.

Cade and I have been best friends since we were ten years old. We've gone through all the important stages of life together. We both played hockey for the University of Michigan and were drafted to the Cranes upon graduation. Some might say our friendship could use a few more boundaries, but we're fine just the way we are. Now that he's dating my sister, our lives are even more entwined, and I don't see that changing.

"He's parking the car. He dropped me off at the door so I could get up here," she says. "He'll be here soon."

I nod, and I know I'm radiating pure worry by the look on Iris's face. It's impossible not to. In a matter of minutes, I'll find out the course of my future, and if it's worst-case scenario, I truly don't know what I'll do. I can't imagine a life without hockey. Obviously, I can't play forever, but at twenty-six, I'm way too young for retirement.

"Everything's going to be okay." Iris pulls up a chair next to Mom and takes a seat at my bedside.

I don't normally shy away from attention, but all this fixating over my injury and the sympathy in their eyes are more than I want to deal with. I gesture toward the jersey she's wearing in an attempt to change the subject. Cade's number, the number ten, is front and center across her chest. "Traitor." My eyes narrow.

She drops her chin, looking at her jersey. The skin around her eyes crinkle. "I'm sorry. I had to. He's my boyfriend, but I made a sign with both of your numbers."

"Yeah, I saw your sign," I grumble. "I'm just saying, you think your sister loves you, and then she's discarding your jersey for someone else's as if it means nothing."

She laughs. "You can have every female NHL fan in Michigan wear your number. Cade has me."

I extend my hand to Mom, who's wearing the number eighteen on her chest. "At least my mom still loves me."

"Always." She squeezes my hand.

A ton of females in the stands today had number eighteen jerseys on. I can't deny that. It's a running joke that my number is also a contract. Must be at least eighteen years old to win the affection of Beckett Feldmore. I'm not about to get tangled up with a sixteen-year-old who looks twenty-one. No thank you. I may be a slut, but there's a line I won't cross—for moral and legal reasons. I play it off like that was the reason I chose the number in the first place. The truth is much less exciting. When Cade and I were drafted and asked what number we wanted, he immediately knew he wanted to be ten, as it had special meaning to him. I hadn't thought about it, and my number from college was already taken. The equipment manager had looked at me and said, "Eighteen is available," and I agreed. The made-up age of consent story is just better.

Two people enter my room. One I know well but wish I didn't, and the other I've never seen before but wish I knew intimately.

Our team doctor, Dr. Hoomeister, better known as Hootie, waddles in. The man is ancient, grossly incompetent, and looks like an owl. I swear he knows some scandalous secret about Coach Albright or the team owner that he holds over their heads because there is no other reason he should be the doctor to an NHL team. I wouldn't trust the man to water my plants, let alone hold any authority over my medical care. Thankfully, the team's PTs are brilliant, so I've gone to them any time I've needed anything over the past four years.

The woman at his side is stunning. She's tall and slender with beautiful curves. She has long brown hair that falls over her shoulders in waves, big brown doe eyes, and nice full lips.

I sit up taller in the bed, now glaringly aware that I'm in a hospital gown. I'm not sure who this goddess is, but I guarantee I don't want to meet her in a piece of fabric akin to a dress with my ass hanging out. Not that I have a choice.

Dr. Hootie talks, but I'm having difficulty deciphering what he's saying. With squinted eyes, my stare bounces between the blathering idiot and the mystery woman.

With a smile toward Dr. Hootie, she steps forward, taking over the conversation. I find myself in a trance as I listen to her soothing voice—like a ten-year-old schoolboy just realizing the joys of the opposite sex.

I'm startled by the outburst beside me. "Oh, that's great. Isn't that wonderful?" Mom squeezes my arm.

Chalk it up to the meds I've taken, the crash in adrenaline, the headache, or the fact that I'm channeling my inner pre-teen, but I'm in a sort of daze and having a hard time concentrating.

Replaying the words the goddess just spoke, two things stand out. First, I'm going to be able to play next season. Second, she's going to oversee my recovery.

So maybe today isn't the worst day ever.

# CHAPTER
## TWO

ELENA

The worst thing to be is desperate. One will sacrifice their soul to rise out of that state. I should know.

The guy looks at me with an obnoxious grin. His eyes are focused to the point of not blinking. It's unsettling. I've been working for the Crane organization for an hour, and I'm already questioning my choices. Is this a dream job for a sports medicine doctor fresh out of residency? Absolutely, and I'm grateful for it. Will it kill me to work in a culture of toxic masculinity? Not all at once, no... but I'll slowly die inside, little by little, each day.

Because of assholes like the one staring at me right now.

Beckett Feldmore is an attractive man; there's no question about that. In fact, everyone knows it—most of all, him. I researched the team and everyone on it before the game today. It's not hard to figure out who Beckett is. Yes, he's one of the starting forwards and lead goal scorer. He has athletic talent. Yet game stuff aside, he comes from money, a golden boy who has gotten everything he's ever wanted. He's a man-whore, and his team nickname is Feltmore, a play on his last name.

Felt more ass?

Felt more tits?

Felt more women?

Probably all of the above.

Everything that has gone wrong in my life is because of a man who is too handsome, too powerful, and too fucking cocky for his own good. From my daughter's father to my own, most men in my life have done nothing but hurt me.

I never saw myself working for an all-male team. I suppose I pictured myself helping women in sports. Yet a job like this, with its salary, benefits, and prestige, is a blessing. One that I still can't believe is real.

At forty years old, it has taken me twenty-two years to get here. That's a long time. As a single mother, I struggled to keep food on the table and a roof over our heads. I worked full time, took classes when I could, and raised my daughter. Not a minute of the past twenty-two years was easy. But I've finally done it.

My favorite attending physician at the University of Michigan Hospital, Dr. Ameson, recommended me to Dr. Hoomeister, insisting that I was the best resident she ever had. As the story goes, decades ago, when Dr. Hoomeister was an attending physician and Dr. Ameson was his resident, she was the best he'd ever had. The two have remained close since. And, apparently, Dr. Hoomeister saved the owner of the Crane hockey team's father from certain death years ago, a debt that got Dr. Hoomeister this job, and his recommendation for his replacement, mine.

This job is the result of a long line of luck, coincidences, and being in the right place at the right time. However, everything leading up to it was nothing but sacrifice—giving a hundred and ten percent of myself every day for two decades.

The amount of debt I carry is astronomical. There was no way I could turn this opportunity down. As stated, desperate times...

So what if I have to work with men like Beckett "Feltmore"? I've dealt with worse—way worse. I simply need to hike up my big girl panties, keep my head down, do my job, and cash my paycheck.

"Can you repeat that?" Beckett sits up taller in the hospital bed.

Brows furrowed, I steal a glance toward Dr. Hoomeister as he stares straight ahead, oblivious.

"I'm sorry. What part did you want me to repeat?" I question the injured player. I've been talking for a while and have given him a lot of information.

"Can you repeat all of it? Everything you said." He shrugs his shoulders and gives me a cheeky grin. "I was kind of zoned out."

"I can recap for you, honey," a woman, who I can only assume is his mother, responds.

"No." He shakes his head. "I want to hear it from her." His blue-eyed stare holds mine.

I run my palms down my thighs along my black polyester pants, the fabric doing nothing to absorb the moisture on my skin. My palms sweat when I'm anxious, angry, or nervous, and right now, I'd say I'm all three. Dealing with chauvinistic men will always make me a little anxious, no matter how many hours of therapy I've been through. I'm nervous that I won't keep my mouth shut and behave professionally, which would jeopardize this job. More than anything, I'm angry that I've just calmly and thoroughly explained everything to this man, and the prick didn't bother to listen to a word I said. For all he knew, his career was on the line, and he chose not to pay attention to his test results. I'm not often rendered speechless, but I have to admit, I'm having difficulty forming words.

Pulling in a calming breath through my nose, I plaster on a smile. "I'm Dr. Elena Cortez. I've been hired by the Crane organization and will be replacing Dr. Hoomeister when he retires. Today was his last day." My voice is sickeningly sweet and more monotone than usual, but it's the best I can do.

"Wait, Hootie is retiring? You're done? No announcement or goodbye party or anything?" Beckett looks at the man to my right.

"Well, due to some new health issues, I recently decided to retire at the end of the season. I thought the season would last longer, and I'd be able to make a proper announcement," Dr. Hoomeister answers.

Ouch. There's no mistaking the wince on Beckett's face. The comment hit deep. I'm guessing losing to Pittsburgh was a shock for him, too.

I continue. "I'll be in charge of your care as you recover. As I mentioned, your knee has a grade 3 MCL tear. The good news is that no other ligaments were torn. You're especially fortunate that your ACL wasn't injured. An MCL tear will have you out for four to eight weeks. You'll be in pain for a few days and need to rest your knee for a month or so. After that, we'll start rehab. So while a ligament tear is never ideal, I'm confident we can have you back to one hundred percent before next season."

"Really?" His face lights up, and for a moment, he

looks like a little boy. "I'll be able to play next season? You're sure?"

I smile, and it's not completely forced. "There's no reason you shouldn't be able to. As long as you follow my directions during recovery and work hard in physical therapy, you'll be ready."

"Oh, I will follow your instructions to a T, Doctor." He claps his hands together. "This is awesome news!" He turns to his family.

The two women at his side lean forward, and the three of them circle their arms around one another in an embrace. The sight warms my heart as it's clear these people love one another very much.

"We should tell the rest of the team," Dr. Hoomeister says. "They'll be worried. These guys are a family."

I look at Beckett, and he lifts his gaze to mine. "Yeah, tell them the good news, Doc." He gives me permission to share his medical information, as if he knew I was just about to ask.

"Will do. We'll process your discharge paperwork so you can get out of here. The nurse will go over the at-home instructions, which consist of rest and ice. Do not move your injured knee. I'll be placing an overnight order for a new brace." I eye the atrocity they have strapped to his leg at the moment. "It will be custom fit to your leg. We'll be in touch." With that, we exit the room.

In the waiting room, I repeat the information I gave Beckett to the rest of the team and am met with celebration. The men seem equally excited for Dr. Hoomeister's retirement as they are for Beckett's recovery. I admit I haven't been that impressed with the elderly doctor, but I figured I was just being cynical, as I often am.

After answering the team's questions, I plan to meet Dr. Hoomeister in his office tomorrow morning for the final, last-minute instructions and record transfers.

A ding on my phone catches my attention, and I tell Dr. Hoomeister to go on without me. With a nod, he steps into the elevator. The doors close, and I move to the far end of the waiting room to check my messages. My daughter, Ariana, has left me a text message.

She's attending the College of Veterinary Medicine at Michigan State University, and the lights in her apartment just shut off.

*Crap.*

Taking a seat in a corner chair, I pull up my emails, and sure enough, I find a shut-off notice from the electric company in my inbox for nonpayment. I quickly sign on to the banking app on my phone to discover my account has a negative balance. Exiting, I sign into my credit card app, knowing what I'll find—it's maxed out. I don't have a cent of available credit.

My emergency credit card is hidden in my wallet, behind my license. I keep it concealed, convincing myself that it's not there so I'll have it if there's an emergency. No electricity qualifies as an emergency.

My hands shake as I sign into the electric account and input the new credit card numbers. In addition to the balance, there's a hefty fee to turn back on the electricity. Gotta love how companies kick you when you're down. I pull in deep breaths, willing the tears to stay at bay. I'm so fucking sick of dealing with this type of stuff. A person can scrape by for only so long before they lose their mind.

"Doctor? Excuse me, Doctor?"

It takes me a second to realize the woman is addressing me. I look up from my phone. "Yes?"

"Hi. Sorry to bother you, but Mr. Feldmore has a question for you. He asked me to find you."

I blow out a breath. "Okay, I'll be right there."

She leaves, and I make sure Ari's electric will be turned on before I exit the app and shoot my daughter a text.

Should be coming back on. Let me
know if it's not back on within the hour.
Love you.

Thanks, Mom! Love you, too.

Waiting a few minutes, I allow my heartbeat to go back
to normal before I return to Beckett's room.

The same people are inside, with the addition of
another guy. Based on my research, I recognize him as
Cade Richards, Beckett's best friend and the other
starting forward on the team.

"Did you need something, Mr. Feldmore?"

"Yeah, Doc." His full lips break into a smile, and the
stress and uncertainty present when I first saw him is
gone. He runs his hand through his disheveled sandy-
brown hair. "You'll be checking on me tomorrow?"

"Yes."

His big blue eyes hold my stare. "You will *personally*
be checking in on me?" he asks, his voice all husky and
gravelly.

"Yes, I will personally be stopping by to check on
you."

He bites his bottom lip with a nod. His mouth forms into a smirk, those sky-blue eyes still focused on me. "Good. That's all I needed to know."

I'm fully aware that he thinks he's sexy, but he'll find out soon enough that if he plans on using any of his "Feltmore" tactics on me, he'll be sorely disappointed. I don't find anything about men like Beckett Feldmore attractive. He's just another playboy in a world where their charms have no control over me.

I leave the room and retreat from the hospital grounds at record speed, not wanting to risk being summoned again.

*My paycheck can't come soon enough.*

# CHAPTER
## THREE

BECKETT

With my leg elevated out in front of me, I have a bag of ice resting on my knee. I lean against a mountain of pillows and replay last night's game against Pittsburgh, picking apart everything I could've done better. Our team should've won. We should be moving on to round two of the Stanley Cup playoffs. Our performance, as a whole, leaves a bitter taste in my mouth. We had a stellar season only to throw it all away against a team with less talent.

I throw my head against the pillows with a groan as Cade walks into my childhood room.

He glances toward the television and shakes his head. Grabbing the remote from my hand, he shuts it off. "Why are you doing this to yourself? Don't you think you have enough to focus on without the added stress of picking apart everything we did wrong?"

"You know I'm a glutton for punishment."

"Well, don't be. You need to focus on healing. No doubt about it, yesterday sucked. Hell, the other six games sucked, too. There's no question we should've moved on. No one would've predicted the outcome, but that's sports. Sometimes you're just off, and we were off. It wasn't just you or me or anyone else in particular. As a team, we didn't bring it. But it's over." He sighs and takes a seat at the end of the bed, facing me. "Next season will be our redemption season."

"Hell yeah, it will."

"Okay, then. So let it go. Focus on getting healthy."

"Not much I can do now but sit around," I grumble.

Cade huffs out a chuckle. "Yeah, man. Being injured sucks. Watch a movie, anything but replays of the game."

There's a soft knock on the door, and Mom walks in with a tray of snacks. "I brought you all your favorites."

She sets the tray on the bed beside me. "Thanks, Mom."

Leaning forward, she runs her hands through my hair. "Is there anything else I can get for you, sweetie?"

"You know those snickerdoodle cookies you used to make when we were sick? You served them with warm sweetened milk? I could use some of those." I tilt my head to the side with a smile, my charm on full display.

My mother's face lights up. "Oh, sure! I'm out of cinnamon, but that's okay. I'll take a quick trip to the store and make them. Will you be okay without me for an hour?"

I nod. "I'll be okay. Thanks, Mom. Love ya."

"Love you, my sweet." She squeezes my hand and hurries from the room.

Cade waits until she's gone before he cracks up. "What is your problem, man? You're pushing twenty-seven. This isn't normal behavior." He shakes his head with a scoff.

"Hey, I'm doing it for my mom. She loves taking care of me, and I'll always be her little boy in her eyes."

He puckers his lips and raises his eyebrows. "Rii-ight," he draws out. "So you're acting completely help-less for your mom's benefit?"

"Obviously." I snicker. "She loves it."

He raises his hands in surrender. "Alright, what-ever. Is there anything you need before I head out?"

"I'll survive until my mom gets back," I say with a mock woe-is-me tone, causing Cade to laugh again.

He leaves, and I turn the TV back on. Feeling nostalgic, I pull up the first *Harry Potter* movie. It's been years since I've had a *Harry Potter* marathon, and a viewing will go well with all the nostalgic treats my mom will be making me.

Cade returns, cracking my door open. "Look who I ran into as I was walking out?" He opens the door wider to reveal our new doctor, Elena Cortez.

She enters the room, and I snatch up the remote and click off the TV.

"I didn't picture you as a Harry Potter fan." She takes a step toward me, a duffel bag in her hand.

"He wanted something nostalgic to go with the homemade cookies his mommy is making him," Cade teases. That fucker knows me too well.

"You can go," I grumble to Cade, eyes squinted.

He gives me a wink and exits, leaving me alone with Dr. Cortez.

"How are you feeling?" she asks, dropping her bag on the edge of the bed.

I pull in a deep breath as she leans over my knee to take a closer look. She smells delicious, the scent very citrusy with a hint of vanilla.

"I'm good."

"Your pain level?"

"It's not bad as long as I don't move it."

"And you've been icing it on and off?" She eyes the melted bag of ice that's fallen to the side of my leg.

I give her a smug look, the corner of my mouth tilting up. "Per doctor's orders."

"Excellent." She dips her chin and unzips the duffel, pulling out a brace. "Your brace came, but there's no reason to use it as long as you're resting. When you start moving around in a few days, I'll have you put it on to secure the knee. You want to move your knee as little as possible while the ligament heals. The quicker it heals, the faster we can get you into physical therapy and back to playing condition." With two fingers, she lightly pushes against the skin covering my knee. "The swelling has gone down significantly."

I've never been as thankful for a person's retirement as right now. I'm grateful to be under Dr. Cortez's care. I don't want to imagine Hootie here instead. In the day I've known her, she's clearly a hundred percent more competent than our old team doctor. Not to mention a thousand times more beautiful. Not that it matters. She isn't some puck bunny enamored by me. In fact, I'd venture to say it's the opposite. I can't put my finger on it, and she's done nothing to indicate as much, but I don't think she likes me and definitely isn't attracted to me. She's been completely professional but hasn't given anything extra, no smiles or lingering glances. It's as if I don't affect her at all, and I must admit I don't like it. Especially since I can't say the same thing. Everything about this woman affects me.

I clear my throat. "So, Dr. Cortez, Elena." I love the

way her name sounds coming from my lips. "Since we'll be working together pretty closely, we should get to know each other better. Don't you think?"

"I know all I need to know about you, Mr. Feldmore. You can rest assured your knee is in good hands." She zips up the bag and leaves the brace on the bedside table.

"But I don't know anything about you."

She stands tall, and her big doe eyes hold me in her gaze. "I assure you I'm very capable of providing the best care. I graduated at the top of my class and have exemplary references. I've worked with many knee injuries. You have nothing to worry about, Mr. Feldmore."

I wave my hand through the air. "Yeah, yeah... that's all good. But tell me about you. What are your interests and hobbies? Favorite color? Are you seeing anyone?" I drop my eyes to her empty ring finger.

She pulls in an audible breath and rolls her shoulders back. "I'm afraid that information is none of your business. I'm your doctor, and you're my patient, and that is where our relationship will remain. I'm not interested in being friends or anything else."

I furrow my brows and shake my head with a tsk. "Yeah," I draw out the word, "that's not going to work. You see, the Cranes are a family. I think you'll fit in better and enjoy your job much more if you embrace that."

Something resembling a smirk crosses her face. "I enjoy my job just fine, Mr. Feldmore, and I've never cared about fitting in. So don't you worry about me."

My skin prickles with… annoyance? Desire? I'm not sure. But I've never met anyone who isn't somewhat amused by my charm. It must be the injury. I'm off my game and not myself.

She sets a business card on the end table. "I'm leaving my cell phone number for you. Please reach out if you have any questions. Medical questions," she clarifies. "If you start experiencing more pain or swelling, call me. For now, I need you to rest." She glances toward the television. "Watch your wizard movies, take it easy, and I'll check on you next week."

Reaching over to the end table, I take the business card between my fingers. "It says you're board certified in sports medicine and physical medicine and rehab?"

"Is that a question?" She tucks a lock of her long brown hair behind her ear.

I shrug. "Just putting together the pieces of the puzzle, is all. Trying to get to know someone when she won't give any information is a bit of a struggle."

"Have a good day, Mr. Feldmore." She gives me a curt nod and turns toward the door.

"Elena, please. Call me Beckett or even Beck."

She looks over her shoulder. "It's Dr. Cortez." And with that, she's out of my room.

I don't know what it is about this woman, but she fascinates me. A mature woman, a physician at that, isn't my normal go-to, but the more she plays at being unaffected by me, the more I'm interested in her. I foresee this being a problem—one I'm all too excited to delve into.

# CHAPTER FOUR

## ELENA

Parked in front of the grocery store, I turn off the car. My phone rings. Seeing it's Ari, I pick it up.

"Hey, baby. What's up?

"Hey, Momma. Just checking in. I miss you."

"I miss you, too." That is the understatement of the year. I miss my daughter so much my heart aches, but I know she's where she's supposed to be.

Instead of coming home for the summer, she opted to stay in Lansing, near college, where she's working for a local veterinarian's office. It's great experience for her. The practice is the one she's hoping to get for her clinicals. Already knowing the vets and staff members will give her an advantage when it comes to placements.

"How are all the hot hockey guys?" she asks.

"The hockey players are fine."

"What? No hot ones? I thought professional hockey players were supposed to be gorgeous. I mean, the ones on TikTok are."

I shake my head with a smile. "I'm not there to judge their level of attractiveness, Ari. I'm there to help them stay healthy for their games."

"Oooh." There's a teasing quality to her voice. "So there is a hot one. You're just not telling me. Am I going to have a new hockey stepdaddy?"

My head falls back against the seat, and I laugh. "Would you stop being ridiculous?"

"What? I'm twenty-one. When am I getting that stepdaddy you promised?" She kids because we both know I've never promised such a thing.

In fact, I raised Ari to believe that she can be whomever she wants and do whatever she wants in this life without the help of a man. I'm not anti-guy. I want my daughter to find a good man, fall in love, get married, and have a family if that's what makes her happy. She deserves a fairy-tale life. At the same time, I never want her to be dependent on a man. And I want her to stay far away from the bad ones.

Changing the subject, I say, "Tell me about work."

Excited, Ari tells me all about the cow she had to help give birth. The calf was stuck, and the vet taught her how to stick her gloved arm into the cow to pull the calf out. The way Ari tells the story, one would've thought she was talking about something else, something much less disgusting. But she loves this stuff. She was meant to help animals, and I'm so proud of her.

We were the Gilmore Girls of Ann Arbor. It was always just the two of us. Though, unlike the show, my father wanted nothing to do with Ari. It's his loss because she's the most amazing person I've met in my entire life.

"That sounds exciting," I say.

"Oh, it was, Ma. You should've seen that little calf. Cutest thing ever."

"I'm so proud of you, baby."

"Thanks, Ma. I'm proud of you, too. I know how hard you worked to be where you are. You deserve all the glory that comes with being the team doctor of a professional hockey team."

I chuckle. "I don't know about glory, but thank you."

"We have to find time to get together soon. I miss you too much," she says.

I agree, and we say our goodbyes. I set my phone in the cup holder and start digging through the compartment in the armrest for loose change. My first paycheck won't post until Friday, so I have several more days of no money. There's still a little credit left on the emergency credit card, but I legitimately only use it for dire emergencies. Otherwise, it would be maxed, and I'd be shit out of luck if I were to have an actual emergency.

Counting the change in my hand, I roll my eyes. "What kind of dinner can two dollars and twenty-three cents buy me?" In today's economy, not much.

Head held high, I march into the grocery store and buy three packages of ramen, three bananas, and a dented can of green beans on the reduced-price shelf. That should get me through to payday.

I drop the handful of coins into the cashier's hands, and the woman starts counting them out. Looking anywhere but in front of me, I wait. My stomach rumbles at the sight of the shelf of chocolate bars to my side. Chocolate is my weakness. It takes a lot of willpower not to exchange my ramen for a candy bar, but chocolate won't hold me over. I need real food, not that ramen really qualifies as that either. After she's verified the amount, she drops the change into the register and wishes me a good day.

The early summer heat warms me as I walk to my car. I let the vitamin D soak into my skin and give all the good happy vibes. As hard as life can be, I try not to let myself wallow in the negative. The fact that I came from an obscene amount of money, yet some weeks I survive off MSG-laden noodles, can be a hard pill to swallow. Yet I'd eat nothing but ramen noodles the rest of my life if it meant I was free from their control.

I'm the only child of one of the richest men in the world, Anthony Diego Cortez, owner of Cortez Industries. My father owns manufacturing plants all over the world that make machine parts. He holds the patent on several crucial metal pieces for manufacturing machinery. Whether a company mass produces clothing, hand drills, or cereal boxes—my father's parts are required to make their machines run. He has a monopoly on parts needed in factories everywhere and, by extension, more money than he knows what to do with.

My father has always been a difficult man to live with. He is stubborn and set in his ways. We never had a close relationship. I don't remember him ever hugging me or telling me a bedtime story at night. He wasn't that type of dad. Anything nurturing in nature was my mom's job, and she was the best.

After I lost my mom to cancer at the age of sixteen, my father withdrew from me even more.

In my senior year of high school, I started dating one of my father's friend's sons, Alex. We went to private school together, and he listened to me when I cried about my mom. He was the only one who did. I know now that he never cared about my feelings, only about getting into my pants. When I got pregnant at the age of eighteen, my father gave me two choices: marry Alex or leave and never come back.

I left.

Alex didn't want anything to do with me or the baby I carried. Sure, he would've married me because our fathers would've demanded it, but I refused to live in a loveless marriage. I didn't have to be psychic to know what a marriage to Alex would've been like because I had a firsthand example for sixteen years.

For my entire life, I watched my father screw around and cheat on my mother. I suppose they had agreed on a partnership, for my sake, but shared no real love between them. I knew the power of true love because I felt it from my mother. Her love made me feel invincible and shaped the woman I am today.

When I left, my father cut me off completely. I was his biggest disgrace, an embarrassment. My father has done much worse than having sex before marriage, but he considered me unredeemable. I haven't received a penny from him since. Admittedly, some days were rough, extremely tough. I tried to hide how much I struggled from Ari, but of course, she always knew.

We were poor but happy, and I raised an amazing young woman. I'd do it all again to reach the same result because my daughter is the best thing I ever did.

There are much worse things than being poor, and I know this all too well.

I can't say I'm not relieved that the struggle is finally ending, though. Ari is in college and happy. I'm finally a doctor with a good job. We've made it. In three days, I'll start receiving regular paychecks, and I can leave the life of struggle behind.

Behind the wheel, I pull on my seat belt, start the car, and my phone dings from within my purse. Retrieving it, I read the text.

I have a question.

I can only assume it's Beckett.

Yes?

You never told me your favorite color.

That's not medical or a question.

Will I need kinesiology tape during my recovery?

You might.

> Okay, so if I wanted to order kinesiology tape in your favorite color, what color should I order?

> Have a good day, Mr. Feldmore.

> Come on, Elena. Give me something. Birthday? Favorite animal? Do you live alone or with a significant other?

> I was serious about only contacting me if you needed medical help. Please respect my boundaries. Rest up.

> Have a good night, Elena.

With a roll of my eyes, I toss my phone into my purse and drive home.

I live in an apartment twenty minutes outside of Ann Arbor where the rent is cheaper. It's not much but as soon as I pay off some debt, I'll get a better place. For now, it's just fine.

A white van pulls into the parking spot next to me, and a chubby, ginger-headed man steps out. "I'm looking for apartment 1B," he shouts over the hood of my car.

My brows furrow, and I take a step back.

He chuckles and removes one of his earbuds. "Sorry, I didn't mean to yell at you. Do you know where an Elena Cortez lives, apartment 1B?"

I swallow. "I'm Elena."

His eyes light up. "Oh great. I have a delivery for you." He walks around to the back of the van and pulls out two packages wrapped in paper. They have the shape of bouquets, and I assume they're flowers. Maybe a Crane welcome present? "Why don't you go open your door, and I'll take them inside."

I squint, eyeing him up and down.

He laughs. "Okay, then. Or, I can leave them on the ground outside your door. They're just a little cumbersome to carry and top-heavy. I don't want you dropping one when you're trying to unlock your door."

The logo on the side of his van looks legit, as does his uniform. Not to mention, the guy is five feet five of squish. I could take him easily. Chalk it up to a baby daddy who hasn't met his daughter in twenty-one years or a father who disowned me, but it might be fair to say I have trust issues. My skepticism runs high when a man is involved.

"I'm sorry. Sure, follow me." I grab my purse and a measly bag of groceries and lock the car. Instructing the deliveryman to wait in the hall, I open my apartment door and take a bouquet, one at a time. "Thank you."

"Have a great night," he says before retreating from the building.

I lock the apartment door and set the bouquet on the countertop next to the other. One by one, I remove the paper to reveal the contents. I was correct in assuming they were bouquets but not flowers. One is a decorative display of fruit—a variety of sweet produce is attached to the vase-like base by sticks—melon balls, pineapple, and strawberries cut into flower shapes. It's colorful, pretty, and looks amazingly delicious.

The other one is also set up to look like a bouquet, but it's composed entirely of gourmet chocolates of different shapes and sizes. I plop a piece of milk chocolate shaped like a daisy into my mouth. When I bite into it, sweet caramel oozes against my tongue. My eyes roll back, and an audible moan escapes my lips.

I eat three more pieces of chocolate, all different and heavenly, and stare at the edible bouquets. Tears fill my eyes, and my chest aches with gratitude. My sad meals for the next three days just turned extraordinary. Pulling the paper away from the bases, I spot a card I had previously missed.

When I open it, my eyes widen when I see it's from Beckett.

*Elena,*

*Thank you for taking such great care of*

me. Though you've told me nothing about
yourself,

    I'm guessing you went straight for the
chocolate. Am I right?

    Enjoy.

    I'm looking forward to working together.

    Beckett

"Well, motherfucker," I say on an exhale.

Placing another piece of chocolate on my tongue, I release a contented sigh. Maybe the man isn't awful. I needed this more than he'll ever know. Despite my brain's protest, the guy scored a few bonus points on my heart. Not that I'll ever share that with him. I have a feeling if I give Beckett Feldmore an inch, he'll steal a mile, and I can't give him the chance.

Stopping mid-bite, I frown, wondering how he got my address. With a shake of my head, I clear the thought and enjoy the candy. That's a problem for another day.

# CHAPTER FIVE

## BECKETT

S weat drips down my face, pooling on the mat below me. The timer hasn't gone off, so I hold this plank position though my entire body shakes.

After a month of resting, I started physical therapy this week, and Elena's version is kicking my ass. We haven't begun any therapy with my knee yet because she says it isn't quite ready. The focus has been on core and quad work, as strengthening both will allow me to perform at the level I was before even though my MCL will never be the same. The ligament will heal but will always be a little stretched out from the injury.

At this moment, the only thing I hate more than core work is one-legged core work. Motherfucker. My arms tremble, and I grunt, willing myself to hold the pose until the timer finally sounds. Collapsing into a pile of sweat, I sigh with relief.

It's official, Elena Cortez is the devil's spawn sent to fuck up my life.

The woman continues to be one of the hottest females I've ever laid eyes on. I've supplied the best flirt game I have to offer, and still—she's completely unaffected. At this point, I get that she's not into me, but I love a challenge despite knowing it's one I'll never win.

Oddly enough, I don't mind—playing a game in which a victory will never be mine because the game is that much fun. I'm mildly obsessed with my doctor. Flirting with her is the best part of my day. While she's never expressed as much or given me a real smile, I think she likes it, too. I can't explain how I believe this to be true. I just know it. No, I'm not some creep bothering a woman when she doesn't want it. My flirtatious charm is innocent. Dr. Cortez is too strong-willed to admit she likes it.

After the thank-you gift of fruit and chocolates I sent her a month ago, she's never asked me to stop again. Sure, she ignores my advances but doesn't vocally protest. We've fallen into a comfortable pattern —I make sure she knows she's a beautiful goddess, and she tortures me almost to death. It's comforting in its simplicity.

"Didn't think you would make it through that one." She clicks the end of her ballpoint pen.

My cheek rests on the sweaty mat, and I peer up at Elena. "There is nothing you can ask of me that I will not do."

"I highly doubt that." She scribbles against the paper attached to her clipboard.

"Try me."

She ignores my challenge. "You're done for the day. I'll see you tomorrow. Same time. Same place."

I push off the floor. "I'll be here, ready and waiting for you." I supply her with my classic panty-dropping smile, but it's all for naught because she turns away without so much as a glance in my direction.

As I retreat to the showers, I admit to myself that it would be nice if she could show me a little attention. The woman is a steel vault locked up tight. She gives me nothing.

I'm just grumpy. Half the team is on vacation or golfing—out enjoying their downtime this summer while I'm in the gym working as hard as I can. I love a good workout, but I love doing it with my brothers, not alone. I haven't been cleared for golfing, skating, or drills—which are what the guys like to do in the summer.

Cade and Iris are in Hawaii for two weeks, and I'm

lonely. I'm definitely a people person. Being injured sucks, there's no doubt about it. I have to keep reminding myself of the end goal. It will all be worth it to keep my starting position and kick some ass next season. Plus, maybe the utter lack of response I'm getting from Elena bothers me, if I'm being honest. It doesn't sit well with me.

Showered and ready to go home, I grab my duffel bag and walk through the gym. A gorgeous young woman stops me in my tracks. Fans sneak back here now and again, but the security is normally pretty good. Like everything else, security is lax during the summer months. The woman with her long brown hair and big eyes looks familiar, and I internally panic because though I feel as if I should remember her, I don't. Nothing pisses off a woman more than a hookup that meant everything to her but flees from my mind as quickly as it happens.

I rack my brain, trying to recall if I've slept with this woman. She watches me approach, a wide smile on her face. Yeah, she definitely knows me. It would have to be before play-offs, as I've slept with no one since my injury, unfortunately.

I clear my throat and give her a smile. "How'd you get back here?"

She lifts her hand, pointing her thumb over her shoulder. "Through the door."

Ahh, so she's gorgeous and cheeky. Definitely my type.

She quirks a brow, her expression serious. "How did you get back here?"

I squint, confused. "I work here."

"Oh yeah, what do you do?"

Okay, so I haven't slept with her. God, I'm completely off my game.

"I'm a Cranes player," I say the words slowly.

She nods. "Oh, so hockey. Nice." She shrugs. "I don't watch hockey. Honestly, I don't watch sports. They're not my thing."

"Then what are you doing here?"

Elena walks up beside me and approaches the mystery woman, pulling her into a hug. She turns to address me. "She's looking for me. This is my daughter, Ari," she says before turning to the woman. "Ari, this is Beckett."

Ari nods. "Oh, the guy who hurt his knee. How's it feeling?"

My eyes drop to my knee. "Fine." I raise my head and give it a shake. "Your daughter? You never told me you had a kid... or adult." How can this woman possibly be Elena's daughter? Did she have her when she was twelve?

Elena eyes me, amused. A faint smile crosses her

face. "In fairness, I haven't told you anything about myself, but yes, I have a daughter."

"How old are you?" I ask Ari.

"Twenty-one," she answers.

"How old are you?" I ask Elena, not caring that it's a rude question.

It's just dawned on me that I know absolutely nothing about this woman. We've worked together every day for a month. I've told her my life story, not that she asked me to but someone had to fill the empty spaces with conversation. The good doctor is right. She hasn't told me anything, even the most important parts of her life that one would think should be shared. Hell, if I had a kid, I'd tell everyone. How repulsed must she actually be if she can't even share that she's a mother?

Elena doesn't answer, and the three of us stand there in awkward silence.

After a minute, the daughter speaks up. "She's forty. Got pregnant with me when she was eighteen. It's just me. I'm the only kid. And don't take it personally. It's nothing against you. She's always been weirdly private."

My emotions must be written all over my face because she answered several of my questions, which is helpful because we know my doctor isn't about to tell me shit.

I hike my duffel bag up over my shoulder and give

Ari a smile. "Well, it's nice to meet you." I take a step around her, ready to leave.

"I'm home from school. I go to Michigan State. I'm in the vet program there. Well, not that I'm in classes right now, but I stayed back to work for the summer. Anyway, I'm home for the weekend. We're just heading out to lunch. Do you want to join us?"

Elena's body tenses, and her face freezes in something resembling a panicked expression.

I don't understand this woman, but she's starting to piss me off. She almost looks frightened by the invitation.

With a sigh and a shake of my head, I decline. "Thank you for the invite, but I like to spend my downtime with people I care about like friends and family, and your mom is neither. Have a great weekend and good luck at school."

Without another glance toward Elena, I head out of the gym and the building. All my friends and family are busy this weekend, but I'd rather be alone than be with someone who thinks so little of me. I feel like an idiot. All this time, I thought she was playing hard to get. The truth is, she's not impressed with me in the least. She has zero desire for me to get to know her.

The last team doctor was a complete imbecile, but at least he wasn't too good to talk to me. Hell, I knew his Pomeranian's first, middle, and last name and the fluffy thing's birthday. For fuck's sake, I knew his house cleaner's zodiac sign. He was part of the Crane family.

Dr. Cortez is seeing me at my most vulnerable. I'm trusting her and trying to build some sort of a connection. Yes, I'm flirting, but I'd be happy with a friendship. The woman has given me nothing.

Sure, my ego is bruised, but I can't help feeling it's more than that. Whatever it is, I don't like it one bit.

# CHAPTER
## SIX

ELENA

A ri eats from the carton of ice cream, giggling away as the movie *How to Lose a Guy in Ten Days* plays. I signed up for a streaming service that I've heard people rave about for years. Now that I have internet, the selection of shows and movies is amazing. Ari and I have always used the archaic antenna to watch local channels, or we'd rent DVDs from the library and watch them on a DVD player I got for two dollars at a garage sale.

Experiencing the joys of a smart TV, internet, and streaming services is something else. It's also rather addicting. Now that my daughter has moved out and I finished my residency, I have so much more time on my hands. My only real patient is Beckett. All the other players are healthy and staying that way since it's offseason. I've been spending my hours of free time bingeing shows. The streaming service carries the *Gilmore Girls*, Ari's and my favorite, and I've watched the entire series, from the first episode to the last, in less than a week. I may have a problem.

Getting regular and admittedly hefty paychecks is a luxury I can get used to. I won't always spend all my free time in front of a television, but it's years overdue, so I'm enjoying it.

The movie ends, and Ari looks at me. "I can't believe we've never seen that one. You would think that the library would carry it."

"I know. It's a good one."

"Though, in your case, it's called how to lose a guy in thirty seconds," she teases.

She has not let up about Beckett since he stormed off all butt hurt after he'd met Ari on Friday. I see his point to an extent. But I've also made it very clear that I'm a private person. I don't know why that concept is so hard for some people to grasp.

"Would you stop with that already?" I stand, grabbing the rest of the carton of melted ice cream from the coffee table.

Ari follows me into the kitchen. "I'm just saying the guy was hurt. I get that you're private, Mom, but sometimes you overdo it."

"Setting boundaries is a personal thing. I can't overdo it. My boundaries are set where I'm comfortable, and I won't apologize for that."

"Yeah, but you've been working with the guy for a month. He's a big sports dude and injured, so I imagine he feels vulnerable. He's let you in and told you all about himself to build a relationship so he doesn't have to feel so exposed. A little kindness and bedside manner can go a long way."

I drop the container of half-eaten ice cream in the trash, pretending that the waste doesn't bother me, and look at Ari. "I have a great bedside manner. That's what Dr. Ameson, who ultimately got me this job, loved most about me."

"Maybe you did at the hospital, but not with Beckett. I saw you two together for sixty seconds, and I can tell you're different with him."

I raise my hands in protest, my voice coming out more shrill than I'd like. "I have to be. He wants things that I can't give him. It's best this way for everyone involved."

She leans her hip against the counter, arms crossed as I rinse off her spoon and put it in the dishwasher. "Or maybe you want him, too."

"Ari!" I gasp. "He's my patient."

"Yeah. A freaking hot one."

"No." I shake my head. "I'm way too old for him.

You saw his reaction to me having a full-grown daughter. I'm old enough to be his mother."

"Technically, if you had him at thirteen." She quirks a brow. "But that's not what he was upset about. He was upset that he didn't know you were a mom in the first place. His face was hurt, but he was not grossed out or anything. Plus, you're not eighty, Mom. You're forty. You could still have kids."

I suppress a laugh. "I'm afraid that ship has sailed. I'm too old."

She stands up tall, hands on her hips. "Kids aside, you're hot. You're hotter than most of my friends. And you're young. Stop acting like you're a granny."

"I could be a granny. I had a three-year-old at your age."

"Yeah." She tilts her head to the side, wearing a mirror reflection of my smirk. "Well, I know about this glorious invention called birth control, so that won't be happening anytime soon."

Gasping, I smack her arm. "You little brat." I huff out a laugh. "Had I used birth control, you wouldn't be here."

She chuckles. "Maybe that would've been better for you. God knows our life wasn't easy."

My smile drops, the playfulness of the moment gone. Tears fill my eyes, and I wrap my arms around my daughter, hugging her tight. I kiss the top of her head and smooth my palm against her hair, pressing my lips against her brunette strands. "Don't even kid about that, Ariana. You are the greatest thing to ever happen to me. I have never regretted a second of my life with you. You know that, right?"

She hugs me back. "Yes, Mom. Of course, I know that."

"I love you." I take hold of her shoulders and move us a foot apart so I can look into her big brown eyes. I want her to feel the statement down to her soul.

"I love you, too, Ma."

"Okay." I nod, satisfied, and pull her into another hug.

Eventually, she steps away. "I'm just saying that you're not tied down anymore. I'm off doing my thing. You're a real doctor now, a career woman. You're young and hot and have the world at your fingertips. Go get yourself some smoking hockey boy sex if that's what you want. You don't have to be so closed off and protective anymore. We're safe and happy. You know? It's your time now, Ma. Don't sit around watching hours of television every day. Live your life."

I hold up my pointer finger. "First of all, it would be wildly unprofessional to have sex with a patient, not that I want to anyway." I stick up a second finger. "Second, I do more with my life than watch TV."

"Really?" Ari scoffs. "You know I can see your

watch history, right? You've had a smart TV and a streaming service for three weeks, and there are hours'—no days'—worth of shows and movies in your "watch again" section."

"Well." I cross my arms with a huff. "I did *not* know that. And you are a little know-it-all who should show your mother some respect."

She throws her head back in laughter. "I know things, Ma." She shrugs and boops my nose with her pointer finger. She makes her way to the living room and calls over her shoulder, "I learned from the best. And I know you're into that Beckett dude, too."

I follow her into the living room. "Ari, I am not."

"Ari, I am not." She repeats my words in a high-pitched tone. "Come on, Ma. Stop lying to yourself. You're into him, and he's clearly into you. Live a little."

Ignoring her, I head into the laundry room and switch over her load. I'm fully aware that as a full-grown adult, she should be doing her own laundry, but it makes me feel good to help her. Maybe she's right. My identity has always revolved around taking care of her and going to school. She no longer needs me, and I'm done with school. Getting a few hobbies wouldn't hurt. It might be nice. In the game of survival, I've never had time for something as trivial as a hobby. I could do those diamond painting things or crochet or take up canning? Ugh, yeah... hobbies aren't for me.

Starting the dryer, I head back into the living room. "I'm starting to wonder if maybe you're a little too free at college. You're giving me a lot of sex advice, and to be honest, you're much too young to know anything about that."

"Aren't you the one who just said you had a three-year-old child at my age, which means you had sex when you were four years younger than I am now?" She puckers her lips, and her eyes narrow in challenge.

She has no problem taking this conversation there, but it's not somewhere I want to go. Accusation is written all over her face, and though she doesn't say it, I see it—she's implying I'm a prude. Maybe she's right? The first and only man I've had sex with gave me her.

How did I find myself in this alternate universe where my daughter has more life experiences than me? I can use the poverty, single-mother, going-to-college excuse all I want, but the fact is, I'm scared. I've been terrified for a long time. The past two decades, while real and very challenging, gave me the perfect crutch to hide behind. Now that I don't have anything to shield me, I'll have to face it.

Later.

"I just put your clothes in the dryer, which gives us a good hour before you have to leave. What do you want to watch?"

She scrunches her nose and gives me a smile. "Only the best show ever."

"*Gilmore Girls*?"

"*Gilmore Girls*."

"From the beginning?"

"Is there any other acceptable starting place?"

I plop down on the sofa and lean into Ari. She wraps her arm around my shoulder. "From the beginning, it is." I cue up the show. "Do you have to leave tonight?"

"Yeah." She sighs. "I work in the morning. But I can stay for at least three episodes."

"Four."

She chuckles. "Okay, four."

I'll figure out the answer to life's struggles another day. For now, I'm hanging out with my girl.

# CHAPTER
## SEVEN

ELENA

I t's been a week since Ari's visit, and the training sessions with Beckett have returned to how they were for the most part. Actually, they've been better. Regardless of how mad he seemed at the time, he's let it all go. It's one of the things I really like about the man. He's just... chill. Besides hockey, he doesn't take life too seriously. He doesn't hold on to anger or grudges. He's fun, easygoing, and loves to talk. Maybe too much. I'm trying not to judge that aspect of his personality too harshly because it's hard to get an accurate read when I haven't offered much in the way of conversation over the past month. So unless we were to work together in silence, he had to be the one doing the talking.

I'm trying to be more open and build my patient rapport with Beckett. Some of the things Ari said made sense. I may be projecting some of my own insecurities and fears onto Beckett when he's done nothing to deserve it. I'm trying this new strategy where I pretend Beckett is one of my favorite patients at the University of Michigan Hospital. Because of Mildred's age and her double knee replacement, she was admitted for a couple of weeks. She'd ask me how my night was every morning, and I'd return the question. Simple. Easy. Nonthreatening.

Each day, I visualize what I would say if Mildred were here and striking up a conversation with the hockey player. Beckett was visibly shocked when I asked him what he'd done over the weekend, but he shook it off and carried on as if asking about his life was something I always did.

Conversing about TV shows is something we do with ease. One, because it's the only thing I really have to talk about, and two, now that I'm watching some of the more popular shows, I have opinions. I'm pathetic, I know... but I'm trying. I don't want to be a bitter Betty my entire life. It's just hard to tear down walls that have been firmly in place for so long.

"We good?" Beckett grunts, dropping his leg onto the bench, having completed a third set of weighted leg raises. Sweat runs down his face.

I'm running out of things to have him do that don't require the use of his knee. I want to give the ligament at least another week to heal before we start working it. I've been having him focus on core and quad strengthening, and at this point, he has the quads of a god. "Give me another twenty-five on each leg."

"Yeah?" He grins with a shake of his head. "Whatever you say, Doc."

He starts his lifts with a slow and controlled movement as we've practiced. The upper part of his leg trembles, his muscles fatigued at this point, but I know he has another set in him. The guy is a machine. I can't wait until we can really start using his knees. I'm fascinated by the body. It's one of the many reasons I went into sports medicine. I love pushing an athlete's body to its limit and see how well we can get it to perform. Beckett is an amazing athlete. I don't have to watch him play to know that's true. Not only does he have the muscles and the form, but he has that fire that all the great ones have.

"Excuse me. I'm looking for a Ms. Elena Cortez?"

I turn around to find a mail courier holding a manila envelope. "I'm Elena."

"Sign here." He holds out a digital signature pad. I scribble my name onto the black screen with the stylus, and he hands me the envelope before leaving.

Beckett continues his reps while I open the envelope and read the contents.

It takes me a second to figure out why a law firm is sending me a letter until I see my father's name. Every muscle in my body tenses up, and I freeze, holding the papers in a death grip. My surroundings fade away—the gym, complete with Beckett and his grunts, disappears. All I can hear is the muffled beat of my heart. It's as if I'm underwater, covered in panic. I can't breathe. I can't move. More than anything, I can't believe what I'm reading.

I haven't had contact with my father since I left at eighteen. He made it very clear that I was no longer welcome or considered his daughter after bringing such disgrace to his name. My father and I were never close, but he was the only living parent I had. It wasn't easy to leave a life of luxury with one bag and a handful of cash that I had in my jewelry box, but I did it. The cash bought me time in a stinky motel while I worked as the maid for the same motel. I scrubbed grimy toilets and cleaned up after guests who were so disgusting they had no business sleeping indoors in the first place. It would've been a better experience had the tenants been wild dogs. But no, I scoured through the disgustingness and pushed through my morning sickness. I worked my ass off and saved the little money I was paid until I could afford an apartment away from the slums. I was fierce, determined that my daughter would not be raised in such a place. I was strong... I am strong, then and now.

The letter is to inform me that my father is dying, but that's not the upsetting part. It's the piece of information that comes afterward.

I return to myself to find Beckett standing in front of me. His hands are on my shoulders, and he's shaking me, pure fear in his eyes. I realize that I'm crying. Tears fall from my cheeks in rapid succession. It's not Beckett who's shaking me. I'm trembling so hard my body jerks as Beckett tries to hold me up.

It's as if the wall I've kept fortified for thirty years, the fortress that held my deepest, darkest secret, has crumbled to the ground, leaving my broken soul in ruins.

Somewhere in the far crevice of my mind, I know I should pull myself together. The private person I am would hate for anyone, let alone Beckett, to see me like this. But I have no control. My emotions—raw and painful—are exploding out of me, and I'm powerless to fight them. I feel it all, so much pain, regret, shame... and anger. No, this is so much more than anger. It's blind rage.

Sorrow radiates from every pore, a tsunami of emotions escaping through tears and wails of pain. I'm not sure what is happening to me. A panic attack? Or maybe this is the result of a lifetime of avoidance? Regardless, I'm powerless to stop it.

Somewhere along the way, my knees buckled, and I slumped to the floor. Beckett picks me up in his arms, looks around, and carries me into my office. He sets me on the leather loveseat in the corner and hurries to lock the door and close the blinds to my windows. With a clean hand towel, he wipes my face. I must look a mess, not that my appearance matters at all to me at this moment.

Face wiped up, he holds my cheeks in the palms of his hands and gives me a gentle smile. "It's going to be okay." He swipes a wet piece of hair behind my ear before retrieving a bottle of water from the mini-fridge on the other side of my office. "Drink this." He hands me the bottle.

My tears have slowed, and the uncontrollable visceral reaction I experienced has passed. My heart is still broken, and I feel sick to my stomach, but I'm aware of my surroundings. I'm grateful to Beckett for bringing me in here. It's bad enough that he had to see me like that. I'd hate for anyone else in the organization to witness such a mess. Surely, they'd second-guess their hire. My family has taken enough from me. Memories of them can't steal this job away from me, too.

I swallow the lump of emotion lodged in my throat

and take a sip of water. "Thank you," I choke out on a whisper, unable to meet Beckett's eyes.

"Elena, let me help you." His voice is full of concern. "What's going on? What is it?"

Eyeing the crumpled-up letter to my side, I pick it up. With a sigh, I hand it to him.

He scans the letter. "This looks like end-of-life estate planning for Anthony Cortez. Wait? Are you related to Anthony Cortez?" His shocked gaze finds me.

I nod. "Yeah, I'm his only daughter. I'm surprised you hadn't figured that out already. It would only take a Google search, and I figured you'd done that when you found my address."

He shakes his head, his brows furrowed. "No, you asked me to respect your boundaries, so I did. I got your address from the office. Told them I was sending you a welcome to the Cranes basket."

"Oh, well..."

"I'm so sorry about your dad, Elena. I truly am."

I huff out a bitter laugh. "I couldn't care less about that part. I haven't spoken to my father in twenty-two years, and he was never a dad. He disowned me when I got pregnant with Ari even though he had been the one to push his friend's asshole son, Alex, onto me in the first place. Well, he didn't disown me at first. He wanted me to marry Ari's father, but Alex didn't love me, and I didn't want a miserable life stuck in a love-less marriage. You know?" My entire life story falls from my lips as Beckett listens. Things I've worked so hard to conceal, privacy I fought for decades for has gone to the wayside. It feels as if my body has split open, and I have to get all this toxic stuff out.

"And I was right. After Alex dodged a bullet and the wedding of his nightmares, I never heard from him again. He's never even wanted to meet his daughter. I lost my father and a life of money and security, but I gained Ariana, and she's the best thing that's ever happened to me. But we struggled. When my father said he was going to cut me off, he meant it. I worked full time, raised my daughter, and went to school when I could. It took me twenty-two years to get here, Beck-ett. Twenty-two fucking years. So, yeah, the letter is letting me know that my father's estate and the millions of dollars that go along with it will go to someone else when he passes. I don't care about the money. It's never been the most important thing to me. People have. The lawyers could shred his hundreds of millions and shoot it all out of confetti cannons at his funeral for all I care. It's not the money…it's…"

Panic rises in my chest once more, and tears reap-pear, cascading down my face.

"What is it, Elena?" Beckett kneels before me, taking my hands in his. "You can tell me."

My voice cracks, along with my heart. "It's the person he's leaving it all to."

Beckett dips his chin and reads the name from the paper. Hearing it causes me to physically shudder. "Who is it?"

I release a breath. "He's my older cousin, seventeen years older. He works for my father. I don't want to talk about it, but let's just say he hurt me more than any person has ever hurt me. He stole something from me when I was ten. He was twenty-seven, drunk, and disgusting. He's vile. The worst of the worst. I told my father, and he didn't believe me. He kept that disgusting pig on his payroll. My cousin...he's pure evil. You can see it in his eyes. I can't be the only one he's hurt, either. He deserves a life behind bars. He doesn't deserve to inherit a billion-dollar estate." My tears fall freely. "I've tried so hard to do everything right and be a good person. I've struggled for so long, and it's been so hard," I sob. "But my father wants to stick it to me one final time by crushing me the only way he can. He knows I don't care about his money. But he also knows how much I hate my cousin." I shake my head. "I don't know why he is the way he is. I don't know why he can't just love his only daughter. I don't know why that, even on his deathbed, he's trying to hurt me still."

"God, Elena, I'm so sorry. For all of it. I had no idea you'd gone through so much. That's...heavy..."

Beckett's at a loss for words, and it's a first. My chest heaves with a small chuckle. "Well, you wanted to know me. Now you know me."

He shakes his head and frowns. "That's not you. You are more than the shitty hand you've been dealt. Sure, everything you've gone through has had a role in who you've become, but don't think for a second any of the ugly defines you, Elena. Your choices make you who you are. I know that you're a hard worker. You're a great mother, a good person, and a skilled doctor. You're beautiful inside and out. You're amazing, even if you like shitty TV."

"Hey," I protest, slapping his hand. "I do not like shitty TV."

"The *Gilmore Girls*?" He smirks, quirking a brow. "Really?" he teases, and it brings a genuine smile to my face.

I point a finger toward him. "You cannot judge a show you have not seen. Got it?"

"Fine, I take back the last part until I've verified the statement by watching for myself, but the rest is true."

"Well, thank you."

He scans the paperwork in his hands, reading it again while I wipe my eyes with a tissue. I don't ever want to read it again. It hurts too much.

"Elena?" Beckett lifts his blue-eyed stare from the paper and holds me in his gaze. A small smile crosses his face.

"Yeah?"

"Marry me."

# CHAPTER
## EIGHT

BECKETT

S he gasps. "What?"

It's the reaction I thought I'd get. She was too upset to read all the legal jargon at the end of this paperwork. "Did you read the last two paragraphs?"

"I don't remember."

"Well, it says that if you are legally married by the time your father passes, the estate and all its holdings will be transferred to you."

"What?" She stands and pulls the papers from my hand, scanning the fine print. "That doesn't make any sense."

"It sounds like your father is a controlling man. He wanted you married when you were eighteen, and you refused. Maybe he sees this as one last chance to get his way," I suggest.

Her gaze narrows as she reads the paper. She chews on her bottom lip. "He's crazy. Who does he think he is? We haven't spoken for decades, and he's still trying to control my life? I don't understand him. Women don't have to be married to be worthy. He's so infuriating and old-school."

I'm relieved to see some of the spark return in Elena, the fight I love so much. While I think I handled her emotional breakdown pretty well, I was a nervous wreck. I've never seen someone so utterly broken, and it scared me. I didn't know what to do or say to make her feel better. I just needed to take her pain away. I wanted to wrap her in my arms and hold her, letting her know that I'm here for her. Yet, at the same time, I know how private she is, and the last thing I wanted to do while she was in that state was upset her more by inserting myself somewhere she didn't want me.

Thankfully, whatever walls she'd put up between us crumbled in the midst of her current crisis, and for once, she saw me as an ally and not an enemy. About fucking time, too. I hated staying at an arm's length from her. The task had become my full-time job as of late, second to my training. It's not easy walking a line when you're not sure where it is. I wanted to get to know the woman while respecting her boundaries at the same time. It's not an easy endeavor, considering her boundaries were concealed in an impossible-to-enter steel vault hiding almost everything about her.

"So what do you say? Want to get married?" I ask again.

She takes a step back, looking at me with a shocked expression. "No, I'm not marrying you. Why would you even suggest that, Beckett? We're not in love."

"It wouldn't be real. Well, I guess it would be legal, but it'd be for show. And when your father passes, we can get divorced. I know you don't personally care about the money, but you don't want your cousin to get it, right? You don't have to keep it. Think of all the good you could do with it. You could donate it to deserving charities or build homes for young, pregnant women with nowhere to go. You could start a nonprofit sports clinic to help underprivileged youth in sports. I mean, the possibilities are endless. You could use his money to make a difference, which is more than your shitty excuse for a human relative will do with it, right?"

"The marriage would have to look real, Beckett. My father will have his private investigators watching us. He'll be looking for any sign of deceit. We'd have to live together and act married. That's a huge ask."

"I understand all that, Elena. Let's do it."

She takes a step toward me. "You would really do that for me?"

"Of course. I told you. I would do anything for you."

"No." She throws her arms up, shaking her head. "I can't ask that of you. It would change your whole life. Hell, it would change everything. If we're married, you can't sleep around with different women after all your games. I know your reputation, *Felt-more*. This would never work. I'll find another way."

I laugh and raise a brow. "How? By finding someone else? I don't know if we can technically be labeled as friends, but if we can, I'm your only one."

"That's rude."

A smile crosses my face. "And true? Do you have any real friends besides Ari and me?"

"I haven't had time for friends, Beckett. I've been busy."

"That's my point. I'm it, and I'm willing. I want to help you."

"But why?"

"Because I care about you. You're a good person, and you deserve to be happy. Yeah, you pegged me, I'm somewhat of a slut, but I can keep it in my pants for a couple of months, Elena. I'm not an animal."

"I'm just saying that this is too much to ask of anyone, let alone someone I met a month ago where our entire friendship can be summed up in a few surface-level conversations about TV shows."

"I've talked about more than television. Hell, I've told you everything. My side of the friendship is much stronger," I tease.

She plops down on the loveseat and stares at the paperwork. "This is all so crazy. I wonder if he has cancer or something?"

"You could go talk to him?"

She releases a sigh. "I probably should. We're obviously not close, but he is the only parent I have left. I'd probably regret it if I never said goodbye."

"I could come with you? You're going to want to introduce your father to your fiancé." I give her a wink and my best attempt at my charming Feltmore smile, which, up until this point, has been useless when it comes to Elena. The woman is immune to me.

She exhales, biting her lip. Her gaze drops to the paperwork, and she ignores my comment. As noted, she's unaffected. "Do you think my irresistible charm and panty-dropping ways are somehow connected to my knee?"

Looking up, she squints. "What?"

"I mean, what if it's all connected? My body is broken, and so is my swagger. I haven't been out in a social situation in over a month, since my injury. At first, I thought it was just you who I failed to impress.

But what if I've lost it? What if I'm no longer irresistible to women?"

Elena blinks slowly and stands, her features measured. "Are you fucking serious right now?" she whisper-shrieks. If we were anywhere but in her office where others could walk by at any moment, I'm confident she'd be screaming at me.

She snatches her purse off her desk and shoves the paperwork inside. Hooking her arm under the straps, she looks at me, her jaw tight and eyes narrowed. "I'm going through something pretty traumatic at the moment, and you're wondering, *out loud,* whether your *knee* has magical flirtation powers? Do you actually hear yourself? I'm not attracted to you, Beckett, because you're a fucking child. You're immature and self-absorbed. I've been trying to be less closed off and give you a chance, to be friends. But you and I are vastly different. There is nothing about my life you could possibly understand because of the way you've lived yours. You and I are not the same. We're not even living in the same universe. So, no, I'm not going to fake marry you because it would fail miserably. I wouldn't last a week living with you. I have worked too hard for too long to live my life out from under the control of men, and you must be insane if you think I'd ever agree to tangle up with you, fake or not. The devil can have my father's money. Some things in life just aren't worth the fight, especially with you as my only ally. Thank you for being there for me over the last few minutes. I'm sorry you had to see me like that, but rest assured, it will never happen again. Now, move!" The command is firm and scary, like a drill sergeant in a war movie.

I startle and step to the side away from the door. Without another word, she blows past me and out of the office. I release a frustrated groan. I'm an ass, the whole knee superpower thing was intended to be funny, but boy, did I perform in front of the wrong crowd. I really am a little clueless sometimes. Cade and Iris have told me as much on several occasions, and I've never listened. Fine-tuning my tact wouldn't be a horrible idea.

Jogging across the room, I look out onto the street. Just as I guessed, a man, across the street a block down, holds a camera with a long-distance lens. As soon as Elena mentioned private investigators, I knew her father would have one stationed somewhere to catch Elena's reaction to the news. Who knows how long she's been followed? Maybe her whole adult life. Her father certainly has the money to blow on an around-the-clock PI.

Making a mad dash toward the stairwell, I run down several flights of stairs and exit the building. Jogging over to the parking structure's exit, I wait until

Elena pulls out of the building, then step in front of her car.

She hits the brakes and climbs out of her car. "Are you crazy, Beckett?"

Stepping toward her, I press the front of my body up against hers, circling my hand around the back of her neck. Her eyes go wide. "There's a PI across the street with a camera. Try to look like you like this. It will make our story more believable."

With that, I crash my mouth to hers, taking what I've wanted since the moment she walked into that hospital room with Hootie. Maybe she's right about me. Most of what she said rang true. I haven't had a hard life, and I can act like a child. The fact is, this immature asshole wants the goddess before him, whether he deserves her or not.

She doesn't pull away, and she tastes like sweetness and mint as her lips move against mine. I step closer, my body pushing her against the side of her car. She trails her hands up my chest and circles them around my shoulders. Her touch causes a moan to escape. I've wanted her hands on me for a month now. My tongue enters her mouth and dances with hers. This time, it's my fiancée who moans, and the sound makes me instantly hard. Fuck yes.

I kiss her long and hard, devouring her. I kiss her like she's the breath giving me life. Like she's the answer to every question and the destination of every journey. I kiss her like I can't get enough of her. Which I can't. This kiss is everything, not because it's fake but because it isn't.

Moving my hips, I press my stiff length against her as we kiss, needing some friction. I've never wanted anyone more than I want Elena Cortez. I'd take her right here in front of the parking garage for everyone to see if I could. I want to claim her. Hear her scream my name. I need her body shaking, on the precipice of release, begging me to give her everything, and I would.

I'd give her the fucking world.

But for now, this kiss will do.

I take her bottom lip in mine, biting it gently, and pull my face an inch from Elena's. Her eyes are unfocused, and her breaths heavy. "Let's see what your daddy thinks of the chemistry between you and your new fiancé." I press my lips against hers in a chaste kiss and squeeze her hand before stepping away. "I'm going to go home and shower. We'll get together tonight to go over the details of our relationship. Though I think you should move into my place because it's bigger."

I kiss her again—this time short and sweet—before I turn away, a giant smile on my face. Let the photographer see that. There's no feigning this grin because nothing about that kiss was fake.

Maybe the marriage will be a ruse, but it'll be fun regardless.

Bad knee or not, nothing is wrong with my game. The woman who says she's not the least bit into me just moaned in my mouth as she fought to get closer.

I think I'll like this marriage gig.

# CHAPTER NINE

## ELENA

I've officially gone insane. Let's be honest, it was always a possibility, but it's now official. I have lost my mind. These thoughts scream the loudest as I pace back and forth across Beckett's living room.

He's going on about how I should move my stuff here and get rid of my apartment because a married person doesn't hold on to their apartment "just in case." Truthfully, the apartment is the least of my concerns. I have no emotional attachment to the place I've called home for several years. It's a subpar apartment in a crappy neighborhood. I lived there because it was cheap, and now that I make money, I can afford something else. When this is all said and done, I'll get a better home—maybe even buy a house. So the apartment can go. It's all the other stuff that has me feeling uneasy.

Am I really going to go through with this?

I've done nothing but go over the pros and cons of this arrangement since Beckett suggested it. There's really only one pro, and that's not giving millions of dollars and an empire of companies to one of the worst people in the world. The thought is so maddening, and it's the reason I'm here. I suppose a second would be, as Beckett said, I could do a lot of good with that money. The ideas I have running through my head would cause my father to roll over in his grave. He's never cared about anyone but himself. He has more money than he can possibly spend, yet he's never reached out to help the less fortunate.

It's a concept I don't understand. The sheer amount of money he has is doing nothing for him. There are so many people struggling right now. Just a small fraction of his fortune would seriously change the lives of so many.

My father doesn't know struggle like I do. He was born into wealth and inherited Cortez Industries from his father. He was handed everything on a silver platter. Maybe it's hard to put himself in others' shoes when he can't wrap his mind around what it means to struggle. Yet he's not an idiot, nor an animal. He has higher-level thinking skills. One doesn't have to go through the horrors of this world to know they're out there. All he has to do is turn on the television or read an article to see. Most humans have the ability to empathize with others. I say most because I really don't know if he does.

The cons are too numerable to wrap my mind around. There are so many. A new one pops into my head every second. "What about my job? I can't jeopardize that."

Beckett's blue eyes find me from where he sits on the sofa, completely at ease. The guy is an anomaly. "We can date and marry within the Crane organization. That's not a problem. I think there's a form we have to fill out in HR, and we're good to go."

"But what about my reputation? It's offseason. I haven't even had the chance to work with most of the players, and I'm already going to 'marry'"—my fingers make air quotes because it's warranted—"one of the players. That's not a good look, Beckett."

"You live in this strange world where you think people care about other's lives a lot more than they do. In reality, everyone is focused on their own life. They care about themselves and worry about their own issues. The guys will be happy for us, and they'll move on. No one will lose sleep over what we're doing except maybe your father and that cousin."

Blowing out a breath, I tug my fingers through my

hair as I continue to pace. "What do we tell others? I don't want to lie to anyone, but if we tell them we're doing it to appease my father and manipulate the will, it will surely get back to my father."

Beckett scoffs. "We don't tell anyone anything besides the story your father will hear. We fell in love and got married. That's that. I don't know if your father is as powerful as you say he is, but if what you say is true, we can't risk anyone knowing the truth. If he has access to our phones, it would take one text message between friends to cue him in on the sham."

"I can't lie to Ari." I press my fingers to my temples and rub them in circles in an attempt to ward off this impending headache.

"Sure you can. You've lied to her plenty."

I open my mouth to protest, but he holds up a hand, urging me to wait. "Did you tell her every time you stressed over having enough money for food? Did you let her see your hardships, or did you plaster on a smile so she didn't worry? Did you tell her every awful story about your father and your cousin or, better yet, her piece of shit father? Lies by omission are still lies, Elena."

"No, I kept those things from her to protect her. It was for her own good. I didn't tell her because I loved her and didn't want to hurt her."

"Exactly." He bobs his chin. "Imagine what you can

do to help Ari with that money. You can pay off her student loans, rent her a better apartment, and help her buy a house when she's ready. You can set up college funds for her future children. You can ensure that your legacy doesn't have to struggle the way you did. You can tell her the truth when it's all said and done, but revealing it too soon will only put everything at risk."

Sometimes, I think that Beckett is one of the biggest idiots I've ever met, and other times, he says something that makes a lot of sense and has me questioning everything I thought about him.

I stop moving and turn to face Beckett. Wearing a serious expression, I hold up my finger. "But no more kissing. I know you think that we have this spark or something, but I'm telling you, we don't. I'm not sure if your level of flirting is the same with all women or if you've turned it up with me, but there is only one possibility for our future, and that's an end. There is no us. There will never be an us. We are neither compatible nor in the same season of life. I have a full-grown daughter. I could be a grandmother in a few years. You're young and wild. We're not the same. I'm only considering this arrangement with you because you offered, and you're my only friend." I internally cringe, but it's true. I haven't been the most social person over the years. Friendships were a luxury I didn't have time for. "The marriage will always be fake as will the feelings. It doesn't matter if my father lasts two weeks or five months, my feelings will not change." I pause. "Let me repeat… there is only one way this ends, and that's with us apart. Are we clear?"

"Crystal." Beckett smirks. "Isn't that something old people your age say?"

The way he looks at me tauntingly, trying to get a rise out of me after my big speech, is oddly sexy. I can admit that the kiss outside the Crane building was hot. It felt good, and I was definitely into it. Yet the truth is, I haven't been kissed in over twenty years. It's not a surprise that my body craves that kind of touch. It wasn't Beckett who turned me on—it was the kiss. Trade out the man behind the kiss for someone else, and it would've felt the same.

"Old people jokes will not be tolerated in our arrangement," I utter, giving Beckett the stare that Ari has coined "Ma's 'you better make better choices' glare."

Beckett holds his palms toward me. "You're right. It was in ill taste, but in my defense, you're the one who keeps bringing up the age difference. Our ages don't matter to me in the slightest."

"Well, they should. I don't want you thinking we have a future because we don't. I'm forty, Beckett. There are no more kids in my future. You're going to want a wife who can give you a family. I'm only doing this if I'm sure that you know it has an expiration date. It's not real. It will end."

He sighs. "I know it will end. In case you've forgotten, I'm the one who proposed this whole thing. I'm very clear on what it is and what it isn't. But also, you better believe, if I was engaged or married for real, I'd be kissing my woman in public. I'd be touching her constantly. No one is ever going to believe this if I'm not allowed to touch you, ever."

He has a point. There has to be some aspect of believability. "Fine, you're right. We'll have to act like we're together when we're in public. But it has to stay appropriate," I warn.

"Oh, I'll be very appropriate. Our kisses will be so deliciously appropriate you won't want them to stop."

"Beckett!"

His head falls back against the couch in laughter. "I'm kidding. Chill out. It's cool."

This is so far from cool it's not funny. Nothing about this feels right, yet I'm doing it. "I'm marrying the most gorgeous eligible bachelor in the NHL in the name of money, knowing I'll leave him in the end—is a sentence I'd never thought I'd say."

Beckett jumps up from the sofa with a pump of his fist. "So we're doing it? We're getting married?"

My cheeks puff out as I release air from my puckered lips. "Yeah, I guess we are."

He closes the distance between us and wraps me in a hug. "This is going to be great. Don't worry about a thing."

"I'm glad one of us is confident."

"It's a good day." He squeezes me before releasing me from his embrace. "The best thing to come from today? You admitted you think I'm gorgeous." He winks.

"Beckett," I grumble.

"I know. I know. It will end."

As he says the words, it doesn't sound like he believes them. But then again, I could be wrong. I've only known this guy for a month. I have a lot to learn about my fiancé.

"So we should get started!" Beckett grins.

My stomach flips in utter terror or sheer delight, I'm not sure—no, it's definitely terror. We have a lot to do to get this fake marriage underway, and I'm not ready. But I guess with these things, one never is.

# CHAPTER
## TEN

BECKETT

"For as poor as you said you were, you sure have a lot of stuff." I hike the last box up and take a look around the empty apartment, thankful we're finally done.

"It's not hard to acquire things over the course of twenty years, and the thing about not having much is you never throw things out, afraid that you'll need it someday. You keep everything because you won't have money to buy it again if you need it later. You act like I was a hoarder," she calls over her shoulder, pushing back a laugh. She takes a final stroll through the tiny place.

The apartment was clean, stylish, and organized, just as I imagined Elena Cortez's home to be. More than anything, I'm surprised it's taken us all day to move her. "I just don't know where all this stuff was stored. This isn't a big place."

She emerges from the back bedroom. "When you don't have a lot of space, you get very crafty when storing things."

The bottom line is I allotted a couple of hours of my day to move Elena into my place—an error on my part. I've only moved twice, but I used a moving company both times, which could be another reason for my misperception. Why didn't I pay for a moving company today?

She squints. "You look annoyed."

I shake my head. "No, I didn't realize it would take this long is all. I was going to go to the Tigers game tonight with some of the guys, but they've left."

Baseball isn't my favorite sport to watch. It's much too slow and tame for my liking, but I try to support all the local sports teams regardless. Tonight was less about seeing the Detroit Tigers play and more about hanging with the guys. I've been stuck in my own little world, training my body and knee to get back into shape. I've seen a lot less of the guys than I normally do.

"I haven't even moved in, and you regret it already."

I groan, letting my head fall back. "Would you stop that already?"

With the last box in my grasp, I head out to the moving truck Elena rented. I have no desire to argue with her, yet again, about my choices. She's sure I'm going to regret this fake marriage. I wouldn't have offered if I wasn't sure. Elena's a good person, and she needs help. I saw a solution, and I offered. End of story. Though, if I have to spend the entirety of this "marriage" convincing her I don't regret it, it will get real old real quick. I've never been married, but I'd guess that married couples who spend more time fighting than making love aren't that happy. Since Elena has made it very clear there will be no sex, I'm starting to get mildly nervous about the whole ordeal. We argue a lot.

Yet one thing that has always been true about me is that I do what I say I'm going to do, and I'm fiercely loyal. I made a promise to Elena, and I won't go back on my word.

She joins me at the truck. "That's it. We just have to swing by the office to drop off my key."

"Okay, let's do it."

Elena puts the apartment key in a drop box outside the little hut-like office. It looks more like a storage shed than an office building, but she's not checking out of The Grand. As we drive away from the complex, I'm relieved to see it in my rearview mirror. I look over at Elena and smile. I'm glad she's out of that place and wish she'd never had to live there to begin with.

We pull into the storage facility and unlock the garage-like space she rented. Putting most of her things in storage seemed like the best idea. My condo is fully furnished and decorated. Besides her personal items and clothes, it didn't make sense to move the rest in. Especially since she'll be moving back out as soon as her old man is gone.

When we've finished securing the last twenty years of her life in the storage unit and returned the moving van, I plop into the front seat of my car with a sigh. "What a long day."

"Moving is never fun," she agrees.

I twist my head toward her. "What do you want to do now? We can stop by your father's house. Make it official?"

"No. I made an appointment with his lawyers to get together next week. We can't stop by unannounced."

"Why not? He didn't announce or give you any warning whatsoever that he was going to drop that bombshell of a letter on you at work? Plus, he's your dad. You shouldn't have to make an appointment to see him. I stop by my parents' home all the time without warning."

She scoffs. "Your parents and mine are vastly different. I could see that immediately at the hospital."

"What? Didn't you see my dad sitting in the corner working on his laptop?"

"He may have been working part of the time, but he was there. That says something, Beckett. My father wouldn't have been there. Heck, he hasn't been here. He's never met his granddaughter, you know?"

"No, you're right. I was just trying to say that my dad isn't the warmest guy in the room, but I still stop by his home whenever I want. But trying to compare your father with mine was stupid. I'm sorry."

"Don't be sorry. It is what it is. I made my peace with it a long time ago." Her lips turn up into a sweet smile.

She wears a white tank top and short jean shorts frayed at the edges. Her olive skin has gained some color, moving in and out of the hot summer sun today. The slightly darker hue makes her eyes seem brighter. From this distance, I can see flecks of gold in their brown depths, ones I haven't noticed before. Long black lashes frame her doe eyes, and I have to look away. Sometimes she's so beautiful that all I want to do is stare at her, but I can't because it will freak her out.

And then we'll be fighting, and she'll be convinced I don't know that *this will end*, and it'll be a whole ordeal—one I don't have the energy to deal with today.

"Okay, how about we get some food? I'm starving," I say.

Her smile grows. "I could do food. I'm pretty hungry myself."

I take her to one of my favorite Italian restaurants in Ann Arbor. It's a nice place but casual enough that we won't stand out in our moving clothes.

The server brings us glasses of ice water and promises to return shortly for our orders.

Elena holds the menu out in front of her. "What's good here?"

"Everything." I chuckle. "What do you like? The calamari here is to die for."

"Really? I've never had calamari."

I drop my menu and lean over the table, my stare holding Elena's. "You've never had calamari? Why not?"

She shrugs. "I guess it was never really in my budget. Ari and I didn't eat out much, and that's not something I'd make at home."

"But surely your parents had to have served it at some point. I'm guessing you had some fancy dinners in that mansion you grew up in."

"No." She shakes her head. "My father was deathly allergic to seafood, so it was never served in our home."

I raise a brow. "Are you allergic to seafood?"

"No, I'm not."

"You're sure?"

"I'm sure."

"Okay, then we're ordering calamari as our starter for sure. If you want to dive headfirst into seafood, they have a creamy seafood linguini that is also…"

She finishes my sentence. "To die for?" She laughs. "I'm sorry, but I don't think there's any food on this earth that I'd be willing to die for."

Lifting my shoulders, I give her a smirk. "Then you haven't been eating the right foods."

She grins. "Alright, I'll be popping my to die for"—she raises her fingers in air quotes—"cherry tonight then. I'll do the linguini."

There are times when Dr. Elena Cortez seems so far out of my league in both maturity and intellect. Then there are other times when she seems so innocent and naive to the world around her. There are so many things I want to show her and new experiences I want her to have. She may be older than me in years, but if we ignore the whole MD thing, I feel as if I've lived a richer, fuller life than she has. And it doesn't seem quite fair. Elena fascinates me, and someone as incredible as her deserves to live an equally magnificent life.

I have an unrelenting desire to show her the world. Maybe someday she'll let me.

We order our food.

"So we're telling my father next week. When did you want to tell everyone else?"

"Well, every July, we have a blowout party for Cade's and my birthdays. Our birthdays are both in July, and it's in the middle of the offseason, so it's the perfect time to get everyone together. We started doing it when we played hockey for college, and the tradition continued after we got drafted to the Cranes."

She quirks a brow. "By we, you mean you, right? Cade doesn't strike me as a throw-a-birthday-party-for-himself kind of guy."

She's met the guy twice. I'm not quite sure how she can decipher that about his personality from two very quick meetings, but nonetheless, she's right. "Yeah, they're my thing. But I couldn't throw a bash for myself and not include my best friend when his birthday was a week after mine. Anyway, if I were to get engaged, announcing it to my friends and family at my birthday party would be something I would do."

"I'm sure it would."

I narrow my gaze. "I don't know if that was sarcasm, but I'm choosing to ignore it."

She presses her lips in a line, hiding a laugh.

"That makes sense, right?"

"Yeah, surprising everyone with the news at your party would be something you would do. So why not?

We have to do it soon, though, because we have to get this marriage thing over with."

The server brings the plate of calamari and sets it on the table between the two of us. "We have to start wedding planning, too."

She shakes her head. "No, Beckett. I don't want to have a big fancy wedding. Let's just go to the court-house and sign some papers."

Yeah, that won't be happening, but we'll discuss that later. Right now, it's time to eat.

Picking up one of the deep-fried rings, I place it on the appetizer plate along with a cup of ranch and pass it over to Elena. "Now, many people eat calamari with marinara sauce, and I'm telling you now, that's crap. Calamari must be dipped in ranch but not the bottled shit, authentic homemade ranch."

She puckers her lips and raises a brow. "Authentic ranch?"

"Yes, I am somewhat of a ranch connoisseur, and I'm telling you there is a huge difference between bottled and freshly made ranch. I won't touch the bottled stuff."

"I didn't know there were such things as ranch connoisseurs." She chuckles.

"Would you just dip the fried squid in the ranch and eat it already?"

With a grin, she does as instructed. I watch expectantly as she chews. After a few seconds, she gives me a smile and a thumbs-up.

"Right?" I pick up another calamari ring and dip it in a cup of ranch before plopping it into my mouth. I release a groan, "So good." I finish chewing. "Just for future reference, the rings are where it's at. The leggy clumps some places serve aren't my favorite. I love thick, meaty rings, and they shouldn't be too chewy." I motion toward the plate between us. "I mean, these are perfect. If you order them somewhere else and they don't look and taste like this, they're subpar."

She takes another bite. "Good to know. But seriously, these are so good."

"See? There will be some advantages to being married to me."

"Yeah, you can show me all sorts of new things. It could be fun."

She has no idea how fun it could be, but if I have anything to say about it, she'll find out.

# CHAPTER
## ELEVEN

ELENA

S tanding outside Beckett's car, I peer up at my old home. Beckett's right, it's a mansion—there's no other way to describe it. It never felt as big as it looks right now. At eighteen and pregnant, I left and never turned back. I guess time brings a little perspective to everything.

The expansive home with all of its elaborate stonework has had some updates in the past two decades, enough that when I look at the house, I feel no connection to it. I spent sixteen years here with my mother, whom I loved. I sat at her bedside when she was ill and said goodbye within those walls, and still, I feel nothing—no shadow of nostalgia or warmth from a happy memory. My mind has blocked this place out for more reasons than one. The brain is a miraculous work of art, and it tries to protect us from that which wants to cause us harm. Memories from this place could've sunk me. Instead, my body sheltered me from the pain—suppressing the horrors so deep within my mind that I can't find them.

Still—I tremble. My entire body shakes with nerves. I'm terrified to see my father. All these years later and he scares the crap out of me.

"Hey." Beckett rubs his hands up and down my arms. Despite the eighty-degree day, I'm covered in goose bumps. "It's going to be fine. I'll be with you every minute. We're just getting all the official legal stuff out of the way regarding your father's estate, and then we're getting out of there."

I swallow the emotion lodged in my throat. "Yeah." My voice is weak and hoarse.

Beckett tilts my chin up and holds my eyes with his. "You're safe. He has no control over you. Remember why we're here. Sign the papers so you can do good things with that money. In and out."

My heart races beneath my chest walls, and I feel faint. Beckett leans in, his lips a flutter away from my own. "In case he's watching?" he whispers against my lips.

I nod, and his soft lips find mine. The second he kisses me, my body goes limp, falling against his. He holds me tight against his hard chest. At this moment, I realize it wasn't because I hadn't been kissed in years. It was because I hadn't been kissed by Beckett. His lips possess a magical quality, giving me exactly what I need. Before, outside of work, the kiss calmed me while firing me up to be brave enough to agree to this ruse.

Now, his kiss brings me a sense of calm and security. With each swipe of his tongue against mine, my fears diminish. I work my hands up his back until my fingers thread through his short hair at the nape of his neck. I pull him closer, and he moans into my mouth. The sound causes my heart to race for an entirely different reason.

The kiss is seductive and demanding. It's hard and soft all at once. It fills me with resolve to face what I'm about to do while luring me into a space of contentment I never want to leave. It's a dichotomy of emotions—simultaneously driving me mad while bringing me peace. As Beckett would say, his kisses are to die for, but they also give me life.

I cradle his face with my hands and move my lips against his. My lips ache with pleasure, and I never want this kiss to stop. But it has to.

Beckett pulls away. Resting his forehead against mine, he breathes heavily. "That should convince him."

"Yeah," I agree, clinging to his biceps.

"Are you ready?"

"As I'll ever be." I sigh.

He takes a step back and extends his hand. I thread my fingers through his. "Come on, fiancée." He shoots me a grin, and I can't help but mirror it.

One of my father's butlers, a man I don't recognize, opens the massive wooden door as we step onto the front patio. "Ms. Cortez. Mr. Feldmore. This way, please." He motions us inside. "Mr. Cortez and his lawyers are waiting in the study."

We step inside, and I cling tighter to Beckett's hand.

"Fancy," he whispers in my ear, relieving some of the tension and bringing a smile to my face.

My father sits in his grand red leather chair behind his massive mahogany desk, the same set he's had for years. While the office setup is the same, the man looking up at me with the same eyes that stare back at me in the mirror has changed so much. Only the eyes bear a resemblance to the man I remember. His body is frail, and his skin wrinkled. His once dark hair is a whitish gray. I've always thought of my father as threatening and looming with an undeniable presence. The man before me is none of those things.

I stand tall. "Hello."

"Hello, Elena." Even his voice is weak.

I introduce Beckett, and the two of us sit in the chairs across from the lawyers. The pair go over the legal jargon in the contract all of which is expected. It's the same as the one they sent me, only my cousin's name has been replaced with mine.

"We will need an official copy of your marriage certificate. When will that be handed over?" one of the lawyers asks.

"Soon," Beckett responds. His hand rests on my knee, and he squeezes gently. "Within the month."

The lawyers nod and jot something down before they ask if I have any requirements.

"Yes." I sit tall. "I need this name"—I point at the outdated contract with my cousin's name typed above the beneficiary line—"removed from all contracts. In addition, as I will be taking over, I require that he be fired immediately and removed from all his Cortez Industries responsibilities. His badge and keys will be surrendered, and he will not receive a penny of severance pay. This is nonnegotiable."

My eyes flick to my father for a moment, and I swear I see a glimmer of a smile cross his face.

The lawyers look at my father, and he gives them a stern nod.

"Noted. The changes will be made, and a new contract will be drawn up, effective from the date of your wedding."

The more vocal lawyer stands, and the rest of us follow suit. "Are there any other questions?"

I turn to my father. "Do you have any questions for me?"

He replies with a solid, "No."

"Okay then. Thank you for your time." Beckett takes my hand, and we exit my father's office, leaving the three men behind.

Once the office door is closed, I release a long breath, one I felt like I've been holding for a long time.

"Come on," I say, leading Beckett down a few hallways until we reach the north corridor and my old bedroom. Slowly, I open the door and step in. A small gasp escapes. "It hasn't been touched since I left."

Everything is exactly as I left it. All of my childhood belongings, those that didn't fit into the one suitcase I went with, remain where I left them. I stare at the picture of Alex and me stuck to my vanity mirror.

"Is that Ari's father?" Beckett leans in.

"The very one."

"God, she looks just like you," he says.

I stare at the picture taken a lifetime ago and feel no connection to the version of myself staring back at me. "Yeah, she's definitely my mini-me in looks, but that's where the similarities stop. She's better than me—smarter, funny, sweet, kind, and free. She's amazing."

"She's that way for a reason because she's just like you." He runs his palms up the bare skin of my arms.

"I can't believe he didn't want to know anything

about her." I sigh. "He could've asked me anything, and he chose not to. He's dying, and he's still stubborn as hell."

"I'm sorry." He bends in and kisses my shoulder.

I shrug. "I don't know what I was expecting. Maybe I thought he'd want to catch up a little and ask about Ari or me. Something personal. He just signed over his entire estate to me, and he doesn't want to talk about what I've been up to for the past twenty years? I've never understood him. There is nothing Ari could do that would make me not love her or not want a relationship with her."

"Some people are meant to be parents, Elena. Some people aren't. It's clear where both you and your father lie."

"I know, and it shouldn't hurt, but sometimes it really does." My eyes swell with emotion. I pull in air, willing my feelings on the matter to go away. There's no changing my father, and it's a waste of energy to worry about it.

"Hey." Beckett takes hold of my shoulders and turns me around to face him. Leaning down, he kisses me.

Our lips move in unison, and our tongues dance, and once again—the panic threatening to rise leaves me.

I pull away from the kiss, pressing my lips to Beckett's in a peck. "No one can see us in here. There's no reason for the kiss."

"Oh, right. My bad." He smiles before leaning in and kissing my forehead. "Is there anything you want to take with you?" He looks around the room.

"No, it will all be mine soon enough."

Beckett heads for the door. "So we should kiss again when we're outside, yeah?" The corner of his mouth tilts up in a smirk.

I shake my head with a grin. "Would you just go?"

Beckett's kisses are better than the best calming medications I could prescribe myself. They're seriously addicting, and I might be in a bit over my head. I shouldn't want his lips on mine. But I can't deny that I do.

# CHAPTER
## TWELVE

BECKETT

"Oh my gosh, where have you been? I've been trying to get ahold of you all day," my sister, Iris, glares at the cheese she's moving around on a five-foot-long charcuterie board. "I'm not sure why you're having the birthday parties early. I barely had enough time to get everything, and we don't even have a proper theme."

She looks downright distraught, and I can't help but laugh. My sister takes party planning seriously, and she's very talented at it. In fact, despite being a board-certified lawyer, her full-time career is planning parties and events for the Crane organization.

"The theme is fun, Iris. It's simple." I plop a salami rose in my mouth, and her eyes bulge.

"Oops," I say, my mouth full with the cold-cut flower she constructed. "I wasn't supposed to eat that one, was I?"

If looks could kill. "Fun isn't a theme, Beckett."

I should've known she'd be annoyed. She lives for stuff like this. When I was ten, she threw me a *Duck-Tales*-themed birthday party. That particular TV show wasn't super popular when my tenth birthday rolled around, but Iris and I had binged the series DVDs that my mother got us that summer and were obsessed. The kids at the party were more than confused as to why we'd drained our pool only to fill it with plastic gold coins, but to us, it was amazing. After watching that cartoon, I wanted to do nothing more than swim around in gold coins like Scrooge McDuck. I will say, it wasn't as fun as the rich old duck made it seem. But the party was epic nonetheless.

"Sorry I wasn't here earlier to help you set up. I had some things to take care of," I state, leaving out the part about finalizing plans with my now live-in fake fiancée. Elena and I met with the team's HR today to fill out the Consensual Relationship Agreement. Figured we should make sure our relationship was cleared with the team before we announced it at tonight's party. Penelope Stellars, our head of PR, was in the HR office today, filling in for Mary who is on maternity leave. While I'm sure Penelope secretly adores me, she acts like she doesn't. Her job is to make the team look good in the press. She likes to complain that she's a glorified babysitter to grown men, and to be fair, I see her point. We don't always make it easy on her. I can always read Penny's face. If we mess up and get a little rowdy at a bar after a big win, everyone can tell she's not happy. She wears her annoyance on her face for all to see. Yet today, when we signed the papers, I couldn't read her. In truth, she might have been in shock.

"It's okay. I had a couple of questions about possible themes I might have thrown together at the last minute but opted just to scratch it. The most important thing is that the food, drinks, and people in attendance are top-notch—and they are, so it will be fine." She sighs. "I wanted it to be over the top with an epic theme so it'd be memorable. Cade and I are announcing our engagement tonight. I wanted it to be special."

Oh crap.

"You're announcing your engagement tonight?"

"Well, yeah. It's the first time we'll all be together since we got back from Hawaii. It's the perfect time."

My sister and best friend recently returned from their two-week trip to Hawaii, where he proposed. Of course they'd want to tell our friends tonight. It's a perfect time to announce an engagement and the whole reason I wanted the party moved up so I could share the news about Elena and me.

*Should I give Iris a heads-up?*

"Where's the other thing of gouda? I know I bought more than one." Her voice is shrieky as she scurries around my parents' kitchen like her ass is on fire.

*Yeah… I think I'll let it be a surprise.*

On the upside, tonight will definitely be memorable. She'll get her wish on that one.

Cade joins us in the kitchen and steps up beside Iris. "Hey, babe. Everything looks amazing," he says before plopping a piece of cheese, one that had been the center of a cheese daisy she'd created, into his mouth.

"Thanks." She smiles wide and leans into his side.

I stare at the cheese flower without a center and eye my sister, but her smile doesn't fade. She's in love.

"What are you grinning about?" Cade grabs one of the daisy's cheese petals and eats it.

Once again, it doesn't faze Iris.

I raise my shoulder, the corners of my lips tilting up. "Nothing. Just happy for you guys."

Iris turns to Cade and peers up to him like he holds the moon. He kisses her forehead. "Thanks, man. We're pretty excited."

"Have you decided when the wedding will be?" I ask.

Iris presses her lips in a line, her gaze darting from me to Cade. "Well..." She scrunches her nose. "I think we decided on September. I know it's only two months away, but honestly, we're just ready to be married, and we wanted to do it before the season starts."

"You can do it," I tell my sister, "and it will be perfect."

"It will," she agrees.

Cade, Iris, and I have been a trio of inseparable friends for seventeen years. No one in the world deserves my sister more than Cade, and vice versa. The two were always meant to be together. I can't say I don't feel guilty that I'm going to be stealing some of my sister's thunder today. The shock value of me getting married, let alone to the new team doctor, will be off the charts. Everyone will be shocked. There's nothing I can do about that now. I've made a promise to Elena. This whole thing is already in motion.

The guests begin to arrive and consist of our team members, office and PR staff, equipment managers, and trainers. Other friends have come and gone along the way, but my entire life is wrapped up in the Crane organization. My teammates are my family, and really the only people I care to celebrate my birthday with.

"There they are!" Sebastian Calloway, who we call Bash, our starting center, walks into my parents' kitchen holding two bottles of Barbados rum. "Presents for the birthday boys." He hands Cade and me each a bottle. The gift is a nod to our team's bye week vacation in Barbados, where I became slightly rum-obsessed.

"Thanks, Bash." I clasp his hand and pull him in for a one-armed hug. "We will be putting this to good use tonight."

"How's the knee?" he asks.

"Good. It's getting better every day. In PT and getting stronger."

A large beast of a man, also known as our goalie Gunner Dreven, steps up behind Bash. "But will you be in top form come season opener?"

I nod. "Doc says I'll be good to go."

"Good. Because we're taking the Cup next year. Our showing in round one of playoffs was a joke," Dreven grumbles. Our goalie is always unhappy about something. The guy is as serious as they come and, therefore, the opposite of me, but we're in total agreement this time.

Cade, who is in his in-love optimistic era, calls out, "There is no doubt we're taking it next year, guys. Let's fill some shot glasses and toast to the best season yet."

A round of hollers sounds.

"Did someone say shot glasses?" Jaden, one of our defensemen, joins the party.

The rest of the team trickles in, and we spread out

throughout my parents' first floor. They have a great house for entertaining. Despite having very little time to plan, as Iris stated, the food she had catered was delicious, and the drinks were flowing.

I'm more than a few shots down when Elena texts me that she's here. I meet her in the foyer. She's the last to arrive, and the others are too busy having fun throughout the house to notice us.

"I was beginning to wonder whether you were going to show."

She shakes her head and blows out a breath. "I know. I had to make myself come here. I'm so nervous."

"Well, you still want to go through with it, right?"

"Yeah, I have to. It's already in motion. Right?" She looks at me, concerned.

"I mean, yeah. But we can always stop it. It's your choice."

"No." She stands tall. "No one is getting my father's estate but me. We're doing this."

I smile. "There's my girl."

"Would you stop?" She rolls her eyes.

"Gotta get into character." I give her a peck on the lips.

"Beckett," she warns.

I shrug. "Get used to it, babe. We're doing this. Come on."

The team met Elena at the hospital and of course have seen her in the gym with me as they've come in and out of skills sessions this summer, but no one has really had the chance to get to know her, so her arrival starts a flurry of conversation.

Standing back, I watch as Elena fields question after question from the guys. I tried to warn her that we're a tight-knit group and always up in everyone's business. She thought I was intrusive from the get-go, but I told her the Cranes are a family, and she'd have to get used to it. I'm happy that I've had weeks to prime her for a social gathering such as this. She's handling the inquiries into her life with more patience than she had for me, and I'm proud of her. I know it's difficult for her to share anything about herself, but I want the guys to like her. I don't think she's ever found somewhere she truly belonged where she felt comfortable and at ease, and I want the Cranes to be that place for her like it is for me.

Drink in hand, Bash stands at my side. "So what's it like working with the hot doc?"

"It has its perks." My lips lift to one side.

"It doesn't seem real yet. How did we go from years with Hootie to that beauty? It's messing with my head."

"I know what you mean, and yeah, she's easy on the eyes, but she's smart as hell, man. She knows her stuff. It's crazy to think we had such an incompetent doctor before."

"Are you working with the PTs or just her?"

"Mainly just her. She's kind of a perfectionist when it comes to her patient care and wants to oversee everything."

Bash runs his hand through his sandy-blond hair and huffs out a laugh. "Lucky ass bastard."

Injuring my knee in game seven of the first round of playoffs was far from lucky, but I get what he means. Sebastian Calloway is the youngest on our team at twenty-four, and it can be obvious. Some would argue that Bash and I are on the same maturity level, but they'd be wrong. I've had three additional years of life experience, and it makes a difference. On the ice, though, the guy is far from inexperienced. He's incredible. He was drafted to the Cranes right out of college, like most of us were, and has been our starting center since. We've had an amazing team the past two years, and I credit a lot of that to Bash. He was the final piece we needed.

It's rare when a team has the magic, as we like to say. We have the perfect combination of skill, drive, and personalities to create an epic force of a team, which is why our performance in round one of the playoffs was so disappointing. It's the worst we played all year, and it doesn't make sense because we all wanted it so badly. Maybe we psyched ourselves out and overplayed. It was our year. We all felt it, and we blew it. But as Cade has reassured me many times, we'll redeem ourselves this year. It's true that we'll all be hungrier than ever.

There's repetitive clinking against a glass, drawing our attention to the far end of the living room where Cade and Iris stand.

When the crowd has quieted, Cade tells everyone that he and Iris are engaged and have plans to marry in September. The room goes wild with celebration. Cheers of congratulations sound out as a group of people rush the happy couple. A giant smile is plastered on my face, and true joy fills my chest. Cade and Iris look so happy as they should be.

My smile drops, and I look at Elena, who looks at me with an expectant stare. Shit. It's time.

I hold up a finger, indicating I need a moment, and go in search of my parents. They're often scarce at our parties because, as my mom says, they don't want to interfere with the young kids' fun. I find them in the first place I look, my dad's office.

"Hey. So Cade and Iris just announced their engagement." I step into the smoky room where a lit cigar rests between my father's lips.

Mom turns around, a drink in her hand and a grin on her face. "We heard! So exciting. I'm so glad you all get to celebrate with your friends." She always refers to the team as "my friends," and while that's true, the way she says it makes it sound like they're my little buddies from grade school. My mother is adorable.

"Well, I was wondering if you could join us in the living room. I have an announcement I'd like to share, too."

"Really?" Her eyes light up. "What is it, sweetie?"

I wave them forward. "Just come. You'll see." Ripping the Band-Aid off quickly and telling everyone at once seems to be the best way to do this.

Elena waits for me on the outskirts of the group celebration. I take her hand in mine. "Ready?"

She pulls in a breath through her nose, her lips pressed in a line, and she gives me a nod.

As we snake our way through the partygoers, it dawns on me that I'm not nearly as nervous as I thought I would be. Thanks to Bash and the bottle of rum, I'm feeling pretty good.

I take a step up onto the base of the stone fireplace to get a little height above everyone. Releasing Elena's hand, I clap mine together and whistle. "Hey, guys!"

Dozens of faces turn in my direction. I make eye contact with my parents, Cade, and Iris, who all wear looks of curiosity.

"First, I just wanted to thank you all for coming out tonight to celebrate Cade's and my birthday."

Someone bellows, "Cheers to twenty-seven," which is followed by some hollers and "Happy birthday" shoutouts.

"Thank you." I raise my voice to be heard above the others. "We're truly so happy that you're all here. The Cranes are our family and the ones we want to celebrate all of life's great moments with, like Cade and Iris's engagement."

More cheering.

Cade and Iris raise their champagne glasses and clink them together.

I wait a second for the group to settle before I continue. "And, on that note, there is something else that I'd like to celebrate today. You've all met our wonderful new doctor, and as you know, Elena's been working diligently to help me get back into prime shape so we can take the Cup next year."

More shouting. Chanting. Cheering.

"And," I yell over the madness. Threading my fingers through hers, I lift our joined hands in the air. "She and I are engaged and getting married this month."

Utter. Fucking. Silence.

# CHAPTER
## THIRTEEN

BECKETT

W*ell, shit.*

I knew the announcement would be awkward, but this is on a whole new level. Pairs of eyes blink up at us, and it's completely silent. Our joined hands raised in the air feel idiotic, and we drop them to our sides. I turn to Elena and give her a reassuring smile.

I didn't expect the celebration my sister and best friend received. We've all been rooting for those two for years. I knew the news about Elena and me would be shocking for many reasons. But I wasn't expecting this.

"Um...well...so..." I attempt to address the group, but I'm at a loss for words, which is very uncharacteristic of me. I didn't realize until this very moment how awful it would feel to deceive everyone I love. My mind was so focused on helping Elena that I didn't think about the rest of it.

Elena speaks up, "We know it's fast and may come as a shock. I can assure you our relationship will not affect either of our jobs. Being offseason, I haven't gotten to know most of you, but Beckett talks of you nonstop, telling me what an incredible group of people you are. You're all his family, and I hope you can support us in this new chapter of our lives."

She faces me and presses her lips to mine. The contact completely dissolves the cloak of apprehension that covered me, and I feel like myself again. This is the first kiss she's initiated, and once again, my chest fills with pride. I know it wasn't easy for her to address everyone just now and even more difficult to initiate this kiss. She's so strong and, for a little while at least, all mine.

The kiss is short, and when we separate, I whisper, "Thank you," against her lips.

The guys are cheering now. It's a hesitant, somewhat confused round of celebration, but I'll take it.

We step down from the fireplace.

"Congrats, Feltmore." Jaden pats my back.

"Congrats," Bash says with a half laugh.

I pass Drevin, and he simply raises an assessing brow. I give him a shrug and a smile.

Iris hurries toward me and grabs my hand. She leads us into another room where Cade and my parents wait.

"What's going on?" she asks.

"We're getting married," I say.

My father frowns. "Is this a joke, son?"

"Are we missing something?" Cade questions. "You haven't said a word about Elena other than the fact that she's a great doctor." He gives Elena a hesitant smile.

Iris continues. "You tell us everything. Like everything. I mean, seriously…"

"We know what time you took your last shit, man. Because you texted us from the bathroom this morning, but you haven't said a word about this," Cade says.

"It's not like you, honey," my mom adds, her expression bordering on distraught.

Iris shakes her head. "It's not. Nothing against Elena." She looks toward my fiancée. "I'm sure you're amazing," she says before returning her attention to me. "But had you been interested in her, we would've heard about it, on repeat, every day. You aren't quiet about what you love. Something is going on here, and I don't know what, but this makes zero sense."

Biting the corner of my bottom lip, I look at Elena for guidance.

It was naive to think my family and friends would just go along with this arrangement as if it made total sense. They're right. This isn't me, and if my relationship with Elena were real, they'd already know about it. I just want to tell them everything. They can keep a secret. I've never been a good liar. My mom always said she could tell when I was lying because it was written all over my face. At this moment, I'm trying so hard to school my features and keep them in check so I don't blow everything for Elena, but it's hard.

At a loss for words, Elena comes to my rescue once again. "We know it's fast, and we're sorry to just drop it on you. The bottom line is, we fell in love. When you know, you know. My father is very ill, and we wanted to get married before he passes. He's always wanted to see me happily married, so Beckett suggested doing it sooner than later."

Well, it's not a complete lie.

"We don't know anything about you," my father snaps.

Chalk it up to the fact that her own father is much scarier or the fact that she's just a badass, but Elena doesn't flinch. "Well, I'm Elena Cortez, daughter of Anthony Cortez—"

"Wait." My father cuts her off. "The Anthony Cortez who owns Cortez Industries?"

She nods. "The very one. But I haven't taken a dime of my father's money since I was eighteen. I worked and put myself through medical school. I'm a good person and a hard worker…and I have a twenty-one-year-old daughter named Ariana, who is the light of my life. That about sums me up."

"You have a daughter?" my mother asks.

My father cuts in before she can answer. "How old are you?"

Elena plasters a smile on her face. "Yes, I have a daughter. She's amazing. She's currently in Lansing, studying at Michigan State University to be a vet." She turns to my dad. "And I'm forty."

My parents and Cade and Iris exchange looks.

I sigh. "Can we continue this interrogation another day and return to the group? This is supposed to be a party."

Leaving my family to swim in their sea of shocked expressions, I take Elena's hand and pull her out of the room.

We pass Penny, and she raises her eyebrows. She was the only one who knew this would be happening tonight since she oversaw us signing the paperwork at the office today. "Didn't go over as you planned?"

"Not even close." I scoff.

She puckers her lips and wears a smug expression. "I, for one, am pleased. This marriage will make my job a lot easier."

"How's that?" Elena asks.

I shoot Penny a glare and pull Elena away before Penny can answer. Elena is very aware of my man whore ways. I don't need a summary of my past indiscretions from Penny, at least not tonight. The evening has already taken a shitty turn, and I'm not in the mood for Penny's attitude.

Max, one of our starting defensemen, has a line of shot glasses filled with alcohol on the countertop. "Perfect timing, my friend," he says when he sees me. "I figured you'd be ready for these."

"Definitely." I make my way through the kitchen to the shot glasses.

Max calls some of the others in, and we down the alcohol.

I offer Elena some alcohol, but she declines, stating she has to drive us home.

Home. With Elena.

It's all so weird.

It really is.

No wonder everyone is freaked out. Beckett Feltmore, the slut of the Cranes, is marrying an older, much more responsible woman with a courtship shorter than a wait in a fast food drive-through.

It all feels off. The lying and deceit don't sit well with me. It'd be different if Elena and I were in love, but we're not. Sure, I find her insanely attractive. And maybe her hotness led to me suggesting this whole thing on some level. I'd like to believe I'm doing it out of the goodness of my heart. Yet had our new doctor been the equivalent of a female ogre, I can't say I would've offered to marry her.

Fuck me and my horny-ass dick.

Time passes, and drinks are consumed. I've lost count of both. The room is starting to spin when Elena suggests we go home.

"Sure, fiancée, let's go." I follow her to her car without saying goodbye to anyone. I'm too drunk to deal with any more questions.

Elena helps me into my—I mean, our—condo.

My arm draped around her shoulders, she leads me to my room and helps me get undressed. "Wait here," she instructs.

I sit on the edge of my bed in just my briefs, hands grasping the side of the mattress so I don't topple over. Even in this state, I'm worried about my knee. Falling off my bed and landing on my knee wrong would push back my progress and ruin everything. It's mildly reassuring to know I have some brain cells left.

Elena returns with a glass of water and two white

pills. "Here, take these and drink the whole glass of water. You'll feel better tomorrow."

I do as instructed, and the urge to piss myself takes over. "Bathroom," I groan.

Elena scoops my arm over her shoulders and helps me into the bathroom. She leaves, shutting the door behind her, allowing me some privacy. I'm grateful as I stumble all over the place. Damn, I'm going to have some cleanup to do tomorrow. I don't remember the last time I've been this drunk. Maybe in college? Filling the glass on the counter, I down another two glasses of water before opening the bathroom door.

"You okay?" Elena is there to greet me.

I'm not remotely okay, but I say nothing.

She guides me back over to the bed and tucks me in, pulling the sheet up. "I know tonight was hard, Beck, but we knew it wouldn't be easy."

There's so much I want to say, but I keep my mouth shut. Chalk it up to my complete inebriation or the few brain cells still working, but even now, I know it's in my best interest to sleep these feelings off. The truth is, Elena doesn't know shit about what I'm feeling. She has to lie to one person she cares about, her daughter. I have to lie to everyone I love, and it's a lot. It took a toll I wasn't prepared for.

I can't put all the blame on her. This was my idea,

after all, and it took quite a bit of convincing to get her to go along with it.

Eyes closed, I position my head against my pillow. "I'm an idiot." I sigh, and the thought meant to be internal falls from my lips.

She runs her hands through my hair. "No, you're not. You're kind and loving. It's why this is all so hard for you. You feel like you're letting your friends and family down by lying to them. Don't worry, Beck." She smooths the blanket against my chest. "This will be over soon enough. It will end, and everything can go back to the way it was."

As I drift off to sleep, it dawns on me that her words bring me no comfort. In fact, they make me feel worse.

# CHAPTER
## FOURTEEN

ELENA

Beckett has been quiet this morning, which is unusual for him. In the week we've lived together, he's rarely shut up. There's no doubt he's feeling the effects of the copious amount of alcohol he consumed last night and the lie we told. It was very clear how hard it was for him to deceive everyone he loved. So much so, I wanted to call the whole thing off. Then again, I want to end this charade at least a hundred times a day.

Other than his chatty nature and endless flirting, Beckett is a pretty cool roommate. He's clean, and his condo is beautiful and immaculate. I sleep in the guest bedroom, and he gives me my space when I need it. I thought I was living large with one streaming service subscription—Beckett has them all. Literally, every streaming service known to man is on his television. Our bingeing options are endless. He's on a mission to find me a show I'll openly admit is better than the *Gilmore Girls*, while I'm trying to get him to watch my favorite show. He's awfully adamant about his opinion, though he's never watched more than a few clips of *Gilmore Girls*. Our banter is fun, and the time spent together is more enjoyable than I thought it would be.

As hard as it is to admit, Beckett makes me feel safe, loved, and cherished. Our new friendship is the most meaningful relationship I've had in a long time, outside the one with my daughter. He has this way about him. I saw it last night as he hung out with his teammates. He's charismatic and makes everyone around him feel special, and in turn, they flock to him. People want to be around others who lift them up, and Beckett does that.

I add the fluffy pancake to the plate and drizzle it with real maple syrup and the strawberry sauce I prepared. Beckett declined breakfast, but there is no way he can turn these down. Just the smell has my stomach rumbling. This morning, I ran to the store to get the ingredients I needed for Marcella's famous pancakes. As my favorite cook growing up, she taught me her secret recipe and swore it was the perfect hangover food. At the time, I couldn't have cared less about her hangover comment. I constantly requested she make them because they were amazing. She swore the mix of ingredients did wonders to soak up alcohol while providing much-needed vitamins to replenish those who partied a little too hard. Looking back now, Marcella shared more worldly knowledge than an eight-year-old should probably know, but I still think back on her tenure in my childhood home with the warmest memories. Before she left, she jotted down the ingredients for my favorite recipes in a notebook, which is one of my most prized possessions. When I left home at eighteen, it was one of the few things I took with me.

Plate in hand, I make my way across the living room. Beckett is spread out on the sofa, absentmindedly staring at the television. "Here you go." I hand the plate of pancakes to him.

He opens his mouth to protest, but I cut him off. "I know you said you weren't hungry, but you have to try these. They're amazing. My favorite cook, Marcella, taught me how to make these when I was young, and she swore they were the best hangover food on the planet. And they're delicious."

"You were learning how to cure a hangover at eight?" He smirks with a quirk of his brow, and a sense of calm comes over me at the sight. I've been without his smile for mere hours, and I've missed it.

I shrug. "Much like you, Marcella liked to talk, a lot. Also like you, her conversations weren't always appropriate. In fact, now that I think about it, you would've loved her."

He sits up, leaning his back against the couch. "I may not always be *appropriate*, as you say, but I'm also not talking to an eight-year-old." He scoffs.

"That is a valid point." I grin, nudging his leg with mine. "Now try the damn pancakes."

He scoops up a heaping forkful and takes a bite. I wait as he chews. With raised eyebrows, he nods. "Damn good."

"Right?"

He quickly shoves another bite into his mouth. "I'm going to need seconds."

"Okay." I smile and hurry back to the kitchen.

Pausing momentarily, I scrutinize my current feelings. Receiving a smile from Beckett and simple praise over pancakes shouldn't make me feel this good. Deep within the recesses of my mind, warning bells go off. But I don't have time to analyze it all right now because I have to make more pancakes.

"We don't have to do this." Beckett reaches over the center console of his car and places his hand on my bouncing knee.

"No, we do." I sigh. "You told all your people last night. It's my turn."

After a couple of plates of pancakes and a little rest, Beckett's spirits lifted. Driving to Lansing today to have dinner with Ari had always been the plan, but when Beckett woke up feeling like death, I thought it'd be best to skip it. Maybe Marcella's miracle hangover food wasn't the best idea after all.

Beckett presses the button to turn off the car, unbuckles his seat belt, and turns to face me. "We could do the whole marriage thing without telling her? After your dad passes, we'll get the marriage annulled, and she'll never know."

I pull in a long breath, steadying my nerves. "No, as you said, he'll know. He probably has our phones monitored, and if she has no idea that her mom is married, it will set off his suspicions."

"I know I said that, but can people really monitor phones like that? I mean, I've only seen it done in movies. Who knows if that's even possible in real life."

I appreciate him giving me an out, but it's not worth the risk. "If it's possible, my father will find a way. We're not going through everything to mess it up, you know? If we're doing it, we have to be all in, like you said."

"Alright. Then let's do this."

We exit the vehicle, and Beckett meets me in front of the car. He extends his hand, and I allow him to take mine in his. His fingers entwine through mine, and we make our way into the Mexican restaurant. The public displays of affection are all for show, in case we're being watched. Yet I can't deny I'm starting to rely on the comfort they bring.

The interior of the place is vibrant and colorful. Lively mariachi music plays through the speakers, and I'm hoping the vibe will make the news we're about to deliver seem less heavy.

Ari sits in a booth, chomping on chips and salsa. Her eyes light up when she sees me, and she raises her hand to wave, a wide smile on her face. The moment she notices the person next to me and our connected hands, hers drop to the table, and her smile falls. She narrows her eyes to me in question.

When we reach the table, I release Beckett's hand and lean over to give Ari a kiss. "Hello, my love. Have you been waiting long?"

She shakes her head. "No, we're not doing pleasantries. We're skipping straight to the details. What is going on? Are you two dating?"

I can't tell by her tone whether she thinks the hand holding is a positive thing or the opposite.

Sliding into the booth across the table from her, I state, "We are."

Beckett sits next to me. "Hi. We've met, briefly. I'm Beckett."

"Yeah, I know who you are," Ari addresses Beckett and turns her stare to me. "I thought you hated the guy? Now you're dating? What did I miss?"

My eyes dart to Beckett, and thankfully, he's suppressing a smile and not a frown. "I never said I hated him. Our start was, I don't know, a little rocky. We're very different, but we've had a lot of time together this summer, and he's grown on me."

"Yeah, I see that." She shakes her head. "I mean, good for you, Ma. You haven't dated a guy in...well, ever. You deserve to be happy. I just can't believe you didn't tell me. No call or anything."

"That's why we're here. We wanted to tell you in person," I reassure her.

"Okay, well, awesome, you little cougar you," Ari says, causing Beckett to laugh.

I furrow my brows, leaning in. "I am not a cougar," I whisper.

"Last time we were together, you told me you could be his mother."

I gasp. "Ari. It's okay not to repeat everything I've

ever said. Some things are meant to stay between us." I shoot her a warning glare.

"I'm sorry. That was bratty. This is all new for me. Not only have I never seen you date but I've never been on the outs. I'm your only friend. You tell me everything... usually." She looks at Beckett, her eyes holding an air of suspicion.

He doesn't miss a beat. "Well, now she has two friends."

"I have more than two friends."

"Name them," Beckett and Ari say in unison before looking at one another and laughing.

I roll my head from shoulder to shoulder in a stretch and release a sigh. "Nice. Now there's two of you."

Beckett leans in and kisses me on the cheek. "Sorry. No more teasing. Let's order. I'm starving. Those pancakes have finally left my stomach."

"Pancakes?" Ari asks. "As in Marcella's pancakes?"

"The very ones," he says.

"Wow. She must really like you. Those are special occasion-only pancakes. They have like eighty-five ingredients and take hours to prepare."

I hold back a chuckle. "They're not that complicated. It's not a big deal."

Ari pushes her lips out into a pucker. "No. You're a big deal," she says to Beckett.

He nods. "I really am."

"And humble." She laughs.

"It's the only way to be," he teases.

Ari shakes her head. "You are so not my mom's type."

"How do you know? You just said I'm the first guy she's dated. Maybe I'm exactly her type," Beckett counters.

"Touché." Ari picks up the menu. "Do you guys know what you want? I'm getting the chicken enchiladas."

We order, eat, and chat. Ari regales us with stories about the animals she's been working with at the vet clinic. She wants to adopt a massive Great Pyrenees that she's been nursing back to health after he came in as a stray with a broken leg, having been hit by a car. I remind her to do what's best for the dog. That breed would be happiest on a farm with land and some animals to look after, not in a studio apartment with an owner who's gone twelve hours a day.

"That's a great breed. You'll have many people lined up to adopt him and give him a good home," Beckett states.

Ari sighs. "I know. He already has a bunch of applications."

"You'll love all the animals you work with, honey. You can't adopt them all. At least wait until you've finished school and have a job with a set schedule and a home with a yard."

"He's just so pretty. I call him Bumble."

"After the abominable snow monster from *Rudolph*?" I grin, thinking of all the years Ari and I watched that Christmas movie. It always aired on one of the few channels I could get to come in with the janky antenna I fashioned with some wire and aluminum foil, making it a yearly tradition.

"Yep."

"I have no doubt Bumble will go to a good family," I reassure her.

Ari asks Beckett questions about being a professional hockey player, to which he chats her ear off effortlessly. He could talk about that sport for hours, if allowed.

We finish eating, and when the server drops the check off, I look at Beckett. We can't delay the inevitable any longer.

"Ari, there's something else we wanted to tell you."

"What's that?" She looks at me.

"Well, Beckett and I are… getting married." I school my features in an attempt to look casual, but it's no use. My eyes, nose, and mouth pull into a tight scrunch as Ari shouts to me from across the table.

"What?" she yells.

More than a few people look in our direction.

"Shh… it's okay. It's a good thing," I state.

"What do you mean, it's a good thing? I was home a few weeks ago, and you couldn't stand the guy, and now you're marrying him? It doesn't make any sense. This isn't you. You're not flippant or reckless when it comes to relationships. You would never jump into a marriage this quickly. Make it make sense, Ma."

I swallow. "Well… um… well…" I struggle to come up with the right words, but I have no idea what to say because she's right. It doesn't make sense, and it's not me. I just can't tell her that.

Beckett takes my hand under the table and squeezes before addressing Ari. "We know it's fast, and it seems strange, but it's something we both really want."

My daughter ignores Beckett and addresses me. "You literally just lectured me about not adopting a dog too hastily, and you're promising yourself to someone for life? After what, a two-week courtship?" She holds the sides of her head and shakes it back and forth. "I don't know how to respond. I want to support you, Ma. You know I love you and want you to be happy, but this doesn't seem right. Are you in trouble?"

"Ari, no. I'm not in trouble. I'm safe and happy. I moved in with Beckett, and this is the next step. Things are good. This may seem rushed, but sometimes when you see the right path before you, you take it. This is my path." Everything I've said is true, and I lean on the thin fabric of semantics to hold steadfast.

"It still doesn't make sense to me, but if you're happy, I'll have the engagement to get used to it all before the wedding, I guess." She pushes her uneaten bowl of fried ice cream away from her.

"We're not really doing a big wedding. We're going to the courthouse this week." My muscles tense, waiting for more shrieks.

Ari does not disappoint. "This week!" she screams. "Ma, please blink twice if you need help."

Beckett leaves his credit card with the bill and stands from the booth. "I'm going to give you two some privacy. Elena, please just grab my card when you leave. I'll be in the car. Take as long as you need. Ari." He looks at my daughter, who throws a serious glare his way. "I look forward to getting to know you more in the future. And... take care," he says before making a beeline toward the exit.

"Take care?" Ari scoffs with disgust. "What a tool."

"What do you expect him to say, Ari? You're screaming at us in a restaurant. He's probably a little uncomfortable."

"He's uncomfortable? You've got to be kidding me, Ma. You just dropped a major bomb on me. I don't even have the words for you right now." She points toward the restaurant exit door. "I get it. You've finally started your career, I'm out of the apartment, and you're feeling free, but you don't go and marry the first legal adult you work with."

"Ari," I warn.

She throws up her hands. "I know. I told you to go for it and have some fun. I didn't mean you should marry the guy. He's a child."

"He's twenty-seven… in a week. He's not a child."

"What's the draw? Because he's pretty? You can fool around with a guy without marrying him. This doesn't make any sense." She drops her face into her hands and groans.

"I'm sorry, baby. I know this is a lot to take. Please just trust me. Have I ever led you astray? I've always taken care of us, and I always will. Please trust me when I say this is something I need to do."

"Do you love him?" Her voice cracks. "In two weeks' time, have you fallen so in love with him that you want to spend the rest of your life with him?"

I swallow the emotion in my throat. "Yes, I love him."

The flat-out lie rolls off my tongue, and I feel more shitty than ever.

# CHAPTER
## FIFTEEN

### BECKETT

I emerge from the kitchen with two wineglasses in hand just as Elena enters the living room. She's wearing pajama pants and a baggy T-shirt, and her long, damp hair is up in a bun. Whatever soap or lotion she uses permeates the space, and I take a deep breath. She always smells completely intoxicating, a mixture of pineapple, honey, and Elena.

"You're double-fisting it," she asks. "After today, I don't blame you."

I chuckle. "Yeah, it'd be warranted for sure, but no. One of these is for you."

She takes the glass of red wine from my outstretched hand and looks down at the table, her brows furrowing. "What's all this?"

Motioning toward the poster board and markers, I say, "I thought—especially after the two very awful days we've had—it would be nice to remind us of why we're doing this in the first place. Although, my reason didn't take long."

On top of the poster board, I wrote *Elena*. And it's as simple as that for me. I'm doing this for her.

She stares at her name scrawled across the top of the board and holds her hand not occupied with wine to her chest. With a shake of her head, she blows out a breath. "I still don't know why you'd do this for me."

"We're not going into that again." I blow her off. We've discussed this at length. There is nothing else I can say to make her understand my reasons. But before we get married tomorrow, she needs to feel good about hers. "Take a seat. Pick a color. Let's brainstorm all the good you'll do with that money."

She chooses a purple marker and starts making bullet points on the paper. The people and organizations she'll help pour out of her as she writes.

When we're done, we've finished off a bottle of wine, laughed, and she's filled the entire poster board with good causes.

"Oh, one more," she says before writing *Make a donation to the Cranes in Beckett's name.*

"I think the Cranes are doing just fine. I don't think that's necessary."

She holds my stare. "Job security."

I laugh. "I, too, am doing just fine there. They're not going to trade someone so good."

Now it's her turn to laugh. "And humble."

Standing, I grab the empty bottle of wine and head for the kitchen. "Now, that is something I've never claimed," I call over my shoulder.

"Alright, fine. Well, with or without the Cranes donation, I'd say this is a pretty awesome list."

Returning to the table, I peer over her shoulder. "I'd say so, too."

There's so much I want to talk to Elena about. First being whether she thinks her daughter will hate me forever. But the air surrounding us now is positive and light, and I want to keep it that way. This little activity performed exactly as expected. Tomorrow is the big day, and even though the wedding isn't real to us, I want it to be a good day. There are only so many times in one's life when they get fake married.

Elena thinks we're going to tie the knot at the courthouse in town, but she doesn't know me at all if she thinks I'd allow that. The wedding may be for show, but hell if I'm going to get married in a courthouse. No, I have something so much better planned.

"Vegas? You've got to be kidding me?" Elena's puffy eyes, swollen from sleep, shoot daggers where I stand in her doorway having just rudely woken her up.

"Not kidding in the slightest. We'll be there for the weekend. Pack for three days with long sleeves for inside the air-conditioned casinos, a bathing suit, and lightweight attire for when we're outside. You know how Vegas is."

"No, I don't know how Vegas is, Beckett. I've never been there, and you're telling me with zero notice that we're flying out shortly? I don't even know if I have a bathing suit." She jumps from her bed. "I have some professional attire for work, scrubs, and like three casual outfits. I don't have a lot of Vegas-appropriate clothes, Beckett."

"That's fine. We'll shop for new items when we're there. My treat. Vegas has great shopping."

She paces at the foot of her bed. "Why are you just telling me this now? Why not give me a heads-up?"

"Because I didn't want you to overthink it and refuse to go. I know this wedding isn't real, but it's still a first for both of us, and a courthouse is not acceptable. I've planned everything for us to have a fun, carefree wedding weekend. It's going to be a blast. Stop worrying. Pack whatever you want, and we'll get the rest there. I'll treat you to a shopping spree, *Pretty Woman* style. You have seen that one, right?"

Her face falls. "Of course I've seen it, but she was a prostitute, Beckett. What are you saying here?"

The utter distrust and confusion on her face causes me to laugh. "I wasn't implying that you're my whore, Elena. It was just a reference to a fun shopping day, gifted by your friend and soon-to-be fake husband. That's all. Now hurry up, we have to go," I tease, quickly shutting the door to drown out Elena's protests.

In an hour's time, the driver texts me to let me know he's out front. "Our driver's here. You ready?"

Elena has come to terms with our Vegas wedding over the past sixty minutes. Though she tries to hide it, I think she's excited about it.

"Our driver?" she asks.

"Yeah, our ride to the airport. Let's go." I shoot her a smile and offer to take her small bag, but she declines.

She gasps when she sees the black limo waiting for us. The driver, dressed to the nines, holds the limo door open for us. "You got us a limo?" she whisper-shrieks after we slide into the back of the long vehicle.

"Of course. You think we're going to start a wedding weekend in anything else?" I retrieve the bottle of champagne from the bucket of ice. "Champagne?"

She blinks slowly. "No. It's seven in the morning. I want coffee."

I hit the intercom button and address the driver. "We'd like to make a Starbucks run on the way."

Our driver responds, "Yes, sir."

Elena shakes her head and releases a chuckle. "This is too much, Beck. Seriously."

"My bride deserves the world."

A little over an hour later, we're sitting in first class seats as the plane ascends into the sky. Elena's face is glued to the window as she narrates everything she sees. She oohs and aahs over the city below as it gets smaller and goes on about the fluffy clouds.

She's incredibly adorable, and I can't seem to wipe the smile from my face. It doesn't take a lot to make Elena happy. This woman is the daughter of one of the richest men in the world. She's a well-respected sports medicine doctor. She raised a daughter who is intelligent, caring, and kind—granted, that assessment has nothing to do with her feelings about me at the moment. She's lived thirteen more years than I have, yet she's barely lived at all. She hasn't been on a plane since she was a child nor has she left the state. Every day, she experiences something new that she hasn't been exposed to due to lack of time, money, or opportunity.

The two of us have lived vastly different lives.

Elena did what she had to do. She put her daughter first and her education second, leaving time for little else. She has lived her adult life without many things I take for granted, things I don't think twice about. Being around her makes me analyze my own life and, admittedly, exhibit more gratitude. At the same time, her naivete makes me feel things—feelings I have no right to. I want to show her the world and give her all the experiences she's never had because she deserves them.

I only have her for a short while, but in that time, I'll show her everything I can.

Once the plane levels off with the clouds below us, Elena sits back in her seat. "Fine, you're right. This is fun."

I laugh. "Is Elena Cortez admitting that I'm right?"

She shrugs and gives me a smirk.

"Just wait. We haven't even made it to the destination yet."

She turns in her seat to face me. "I know you love the whole surprise thing, but you know I'm a planner. I've already jumped in a limo and onto a plane with you. Can you give me details about what we'll be doing this weekend? Please?" She smiles sweetly. If only she knew what that simple act did to me. A grin and a little pleading and I'm powerless against her.

"Well, today is all about you. I have a spa day

planned—mani, pedi, facial, massage—the works. Then you'll make a stop at the boutique and pick out your wedding attire before heading to your hair and makeup appointment. After all that, we have an appointment with Elvis at the chapel." I wink.

"Elvis is marrying us?"

"Can you really get married in Vegas without Elvis? I think not."

She giggles. "You've really planned this all out, haven't you?"

"You should know, Elena. I never do anything small."

She sits back in her seat. "Yeah, I see that. Where are we staying?"

"I got us a suite at the Venetian. You'll love it. It's my favorite place to stay. Walking through the interior makes you feel like you're in Venice. There's even a replica of the Grand Canal with gondola rides. And the food….Oh my God, so good. They import most of the ingredients from Italy, so it all tastes authentic."

"So if we're getting married tonight, what will we do for the rest of the weekend?"

"Whatever you want. We could casino hop and gamble, go see shows, explore the city, or sit by the pool and relax. I mean, it's your vacation. We'll do whatever sounds fun to you. I've been there a lot, so it doesn't matter to me. I want you to have a great time.

This whole thing has been stressful for you, and I'm sure you were freaking out about going to the courthouse today. So I wanted to make it fun. If we're going through with it, we might as well have fun with it, right?"

She takes my hand in hers. The contact causes my blood to pump harder. Besides our few "for show" kisses, I've been very careful not to touch Elena, especially now that we live together. I've never done anything like this, but I have to imagine that clear boundaries are important for it to be successful.

"You're the sweetest, Beckett." Her hand squeezes mine. "If I had to fake marry someone, I'm glad it was you. I just want to thank you for this beautiful weekend. It means so much to me."

"We're not there yet."

"I know, but it's already special, and I have you to thank for that."

Leaning my head against the seat, I hold her stare. "You don't have to thank me. I'd do anything for you."

*And that's the truth.*

# CHAPTER
## SIXTEEN

ELENA

S tanding in front of the full-length mirror, I take in my appearance, and tears spring to my eyes. I look stunning. There is no other way to put it. I've felt like a princess all day. The staff at the salon has catered to my every need, making sure that every inch of my body is pampered to perfection. I chose a white cocktail dress, simple and elegant. My hair has been deep conditioned and curled in big waves, framing a face that looks young and happy. The makeup artist, a true genius, applied minimal products while highlighting all my features in the most attractive ways. I hope to look this good if I ever have a real wedding someday.

The sound of a throat clearing gets my attention,

and I turn around to find Beckett looking gorgeous in an expensive navy-blue suit.

"Wow." His bright blue eyes trail my body. "You look fucking amazing."

"So do you." His brown hair with strands of golden highlights falls in a perfectly disheveled mess, that look that says, *I just stepped out of the shower looking like this,* when, in reality, he probably fussed over and used a lot of product on his hair to achieve such a look. He hasn't shaved, so his face is covered in a short stubble, which somehow increases his sex appeal ten times over. He bites his full bottom lip, his chest rising with heavy breaths.

"You ready for this?" he asks, bending his elbow.

I slide my arm through his. "As ready as I'll ever be."

He leads us out of the building and toward an antique bubble-gum pink convertible. It's the most adorable vehicle I've seen. The top is down, and the leather interior matches the hue of the exterior. The whitewall tires are pristine. "Oh my gosh! Is that for us?"

"Sure is. It's a 1956 Ford Thunderbird. If we're going to meet Elvis, we're doing it in style. Don't worry, the chapel is close, and I'll go slow so I don't mess your hair."

I giggle, smiling wide. "I don't care about my hair. This is amazing, Beck."

He hurries around the car to open my door, and I slide onto the pink leather seats. I explore the old-fashioned interior with my hands. All the parts and knobs are probably close to seventy years old, yet they shine like new. The owner of this car takes great care of it. It must cost a fortune to rent.

Beckett gets in, starts the car, and takes hold of the big black steering wheel. "Let's do this."

Extending my freshly manicured hand out past the open window, my hand dips in the breeze as we drive down the Vegas Strip. It's full of life, colors, lights, and sounds, making me feel alive. Beckett turned something I was dreading into an adventure, and I'm so grateful he did. Today has been incredible.

We pull into the parking lot of the little white chapel, and Beckett tells me to stay put. He exits, jogs around the front of the car, and opens my door. He extends his hand, and I take it, accepting his help out of the car.

The interior of the chapel isn't as cute as the exterior. It's outdated and gaudy, with bright red carpet. It's quite ugly, but I find the decor's abrasiveness adds to the charm of the place.

A woman named Molly instructs us to fill out the paperwork that will make the marriage legal. She goes over the wedding procedure itself, which takes no more than twenty seconds to explain. Weddings here are no fuss. "Okay, and you booked the deluxe wedding, so you'll receive a video and picture package."

I look at Beckett, and he shrugs. "I'm sure your dad will want pictures of his only daughter's big day."

This wedding isn't in the same universe as the agreed-upon courthouse wedding, but I can't complain. The truth is, someday, when I'm old and rocking on a swing with my grandbabies on the porch of my mansion that I purchased with my late father's money, I'll want to look back on the crazy stunt I pulled to get there.

Molly continues. "In addition, your package comes with flowers, so go ahead and choose your bouquet from the cooler over there." She points toward a wall of fresh bouquets behind a glass door.

I scan the entire wall of flowers and finally choose a bouquet made of white lilies with light pink accents. Bringing the bouquet to my nose, I inhale. Lilies have the best scent and remind me of my mom. They were her favorite flower. When I turn around, Beckett is no longer in the lobby.

"You're all set. Time to walk down the aisle," Molly instructs and points at the double doors that lead to the chapel.

"Oh okay. Do I just start walking?"

"One second." She fiddles with a knob on the sound system. The song "Going to the Chapel of Love" by the Dixie Cups starts playing. "You're all set. Anytime you're ready."

My head falls back in a laugh. "Oh, Beckett." I grin as I start down the aisle.

Beckett and Elvis wait for me at the end, and the closer I get to them, the more my smile grows. The music stops, and Elvis belts out in a sultry singing voice, "It's now or never…" He looks at the pair of us and says, "Follow that dream! Don't be cruel. This isn't a one-sided love affair."

Looking at Beckett, I press my lips in a line, trying not to laugh. Elvis is throwing together his song titles in an attempt at a comedic performance, I hope. He's either trying to make us laugh, or the impersonator is delusional.

He continues. "I think my 1958 hit says it best, now look each other in the eyes and repeat after me. I want you." He motions for us to repeat.

"I want you," Beckett and I say in unison.

Elvis continues. "I need you."

"I need you," we repeat.

"Finally, I love you!" Elvis dips to his knee in an odd re-creation of a move the late singer used to do.

I look at Beckett and want to giggle, but his face is serious. "I love you," he says.

My stare darts to the plump guy, with only the vaguest resemblance to the late singer, marrying us. He's leaning back, and the verdict is out whether he's doing yet another dance move or if he's having some sort of back spasm.

I return my attention to Beckett. "I love you," I say the last line of Elvis's prescribed vows.

We exchange rings, some simple silver-plated bands that Beckett picked up in the hotel gift shop.

"I now pronounce you husband and wife," Elvis cheers.

The entire ceremony only lasted a couple of minutes, and at the same time, I feel as if I waited for this moment my entire life.

Elvis does some pelvic thrusts and jerks his arm over his belly like he's playing an air guitar and says, "Now, a little less conversation. Kiss the bride!"

Beckett leans in and gives me a peck on the lips.

"What was that?" Elvis steps back in a snarl. "That was not what I call a hunk of burning love. Do it again and this time I want to be all shook up."

Beckett chuckles and takes a step toward me. He cups my face, leaning in a second time. Only this kiss is so different from the first. As his tongue enters my mouth, the chapel is filled with music as the real Elvis sings, "Can't Help Falling in Love." The song, so beautiful, and Beckett's kiss, so intoxicating, have me wanting to melt into a pile of emotional mush right here on the hideous red carpet of the chapel.

*This isn't real.*

*This will end.*

The thoughts play on repeat in my mind because, at this moment, it feels utterly real, and the very last thing I want it to do is end.

I circle my arms around Beckett and pull our bodies closer, needing to feel him against me. The world melts away and it's just me, Beckett, Elvis's beautiful voice, and this kiss. I want this moment to last forever. I know it's not reality, but it's the best I've felt in a long time, so I need to relish it.

We start to sway, moving to the melody, and I pour my soul into this kiss.

My lips start to ache, and Beckett pulls away. "Congratulations, Mrs. Feldmore."

Leaning back, I glare up at him. "Yeah, I'm keeping my name."

Beckett laughs.

The chapel photographer follows us out to our convertible and takes some shots of us in front of the pink car. It's part of the experience, and something I will want to remember. He tells us that he'll email the drive with the photos and videos, then he goes back inside as another bride and groom head into the chapel.

"We should stick around and watch their wedding," Beckett teases. "I wonder if Elvis uses the same script and awful puns with everyone."

"Oh, I'm sure. He's not very clever. Where did he disappear to anyway?"

"I think he went out back for a smoke before the next couple arrived."

"Ahh, well, that's fine. Our wedding dance was better without him hovering over us anyway." I leave out the fact that the wedding dance was perfection.

"It was. Ready to go have some fun, Mrs. Feldmore?" He grins.

I quirk a brow. "If you keep calling me that, I'm going to refer to you as Mr. Cortez."

He shrugs, opening the car door for me. "You do what you gotta do. What should our first outing be as a married couple?"

"I am kinda hungry."

He slides into the driver's side door and starts the car. "Food it is. No worries, babe. I got you."

The expression is so casual, but it makes me feel cherished. I love the way Beckett takes care of me even though he doesn't have to. If I'm honest with myself, it's nice to be taken care of.

# CHAPTER
## SEVENTEEN

ELENA

As promised, Beckett introduced me to the best Italian food after a romantic gondola ride down the river inside the Venetian. The place in Ann Arbor still holds the record for the best calamari, but the noodles here are incredible. All handmade in Italy and flown in, they take these dishes to the next level.

Beckett and I sit on a balcony overlooking the "town square." The interior of this place seriously looks like a scenic and quaint Italian city. Even the ceiling is painted a sky blue with fluffy clouds.

"Do you feel any different?" Beckett asks, taking a bite of the tiramisu we're sharing. "Being married."

I down the rest of the red wine in my glass. "My

head feels a little fuzzy from this wine, but other than that, no. Do you?"

"Not really. It doesn't seem real. Like I know we're technically married, but everything feels the same."

"Yeah, it does." Even as the words leave my mouth, I know they're not entirely true. So much has changed over the two months I've known Beckett. I came into this job with a preconceived notion of the man across from me. I disliked him before ever meeting him. Many of the things I read about Beckett are true, but it only paints a small picture of who the man really is. Maybe I don't feel different being married, but my feelings, overall, are vastly different. I love spending time with Beckett. He's fun and caring. He makes me feel good about myself and brings me joy every day.

This marriage is fake—we're both very clear about that. Neither of us wants to be married, but when it's over and we go back to our regular lives, I'm going to miss his company.

He sets his spoon on the tiramisu plate beside my uneaten half. "What do you want to do next?"

It might be in my head, but I swear my dress is getting tighter with each bite of carb heaven I've consumed over the past hour. "We could get changed into more comfortable clothes and head to the casino for a bit?"

Beckett nods with approval. "That sounds like a solid plan. What's your favorite game?"

I shake my head. "I've never really gambled besides a little poker with Marcella and some of the other staff when I was younger."

"That Marcella sure was a great influence on you." He chuckles. "Well, I'm partial to blackjack. My sister loves roulette. Although the Deal or No Deal Slot machine is addicting, just fun and easy. We'll try 'em all."

"Okay, but we have to be careful and only bring a little bit of money into the casino. Once it's gone, we're done. I don't like wasting money." In reality, now that I think about it, the thought of gambling makes me feel slightly ill. People just throwing away money like that doesn't sit well with me.

"Don't worry about the money. I told you, I got this weekend covered. And don't think about it as losing money. Think about it as entertainment. If you were going to a show or out sightseeing, you'd expect to pay money. It's the same thing. It's just the price of entertainment."

"That's easy to say for someone who has money."

He pins me with a stare. "You have money now, too."

"Maybe. Doesn't mean I have to live like I do, though."

"Fair enough."

The server returns with Beckett's credit card, and we stand to leave. Beckett asks the server to take our picture. We stand in front of the vine-covered balcony with the view of the Italian town center behind us. Beckett wraps his arm around my waist, and the server snaps a few pictures.

We take a second to flip through the photos.

"Sure is beautiful." I reference our surroundings.

"You sure are."

He attaches one of the pictures to a huge group thread with the caption, "After marriage dinner."

"Who are you sending that to?"

"The team's group chat, Iris, my parents, and Ari."

"What?" I gasp. "You're texting with Ari?"

Leaning in, he plants a kiss on my forehead. "Just keeping all the important people in our lives up to date on our wedding weekend. I sent them some pictures of the service and Elvis, too."

"Why? You had no right to do that, Beckett."

He raises a brow. "You want this to be believable, right? Well, if I'm marrying someone, I'm shouting it from the rooftops. To not send photos would be weird. And not communicating with Ari will make it worse. We just have to keep her in the loop and hope she eventually comes around."

"Fine. You're right." I sigh.

He closes the distance between us and presses his lips to mine. He kisses me gently, and the anxiety that threatens to surface dissipates as I melt into his kiss.

When he pulls away, I ask, "You know we're not being watched right now. I doubt my father's PI flew to Vegas to crash our wedding."

He smirks. "You never know. Gotta be safe. Plus, paparazzi could get a shot of us, and if they do we want to give them a good one."

My eyes widen. "We have to worry about paparazzi?"

"Sometimes. It goes with the territory of marrying an NHL god," he teases, and I smack his chest.

"Would you stop? I don't think your head can get any bigger."

"Thank you."

"That's not a compliment." I chuckle.

He offers me his elbow, and I slide my arm through his. As we make our way out of the restaurant and onto the cobblestone streets of faux Italy, he says, "Don't worry, paparazzi isn't a huge problem. I was teasing about that. We'll get them occasionally. I'm known to hockey fans, but I'm not famous as far as the rest of the world is concerned. They have more high-profile people to stalk than me."

"Oh good. That makes me feel better."

As if the powers to be wanted to slap me with a

giant reality call, someone yells, "Beckett Feldmore!" We turn to find a man, probably in his forties, waving. "Is that you?"

I pull my arm from Beckett's, and he extends his arms out, palms up. "The one and only. What's your name?"

"I'm Jim. Man, I thought it was you, but my wife told me I was crazy. We live right outside of Detroit and get to a few home games a year. I just knew that was you. How's the knee? You going to be ready for the season?"

Beckett gives the man his classic easy grin. "The knee is great, Jim. Almost back to a hundred percent. Don't worry, I'll be ready."

"Oh good." The man beams. "That's great to hear." He looks back at his wife and waves her forward. "Honey, come on, let's get a picture," he says before addressing Beckett. "You don't mind taking a picture with us, do you?"

"Of course not." Beckett waves them both forward. "Bring it in."

The wife scurries over, wearing an anxious grin. The man hands me his cell phone with the camera app open, and he and his wife stand on either side of Beckett. I snap a handful of pictures and give the phone back.

"Thank you," the fan says to me before returning

his attention to Beckett. "Thank you so much. You're the best Crane player there is. It's an honor to meet you."

Beckett gives them a wave, a broad smile on his face. "Great meeting you, Jim. I'll see you at some games this season. Have a wonderful time in Vegas."

"You, too. Thank you!" The man and his wife stare at the pictures I took on his phone, talking excitedly among themselves as we walk away.

Beckett continues to wear a goofy grin as we distance ourselves from the fan and his wife.

"Oh, you just loved that, didn't you?" I chuckle with a shake of my head.

He shrugs before taking my hand in his. "As I said…" With his free hand, he brings his thumb to his chest. "A big deal."

"You're insufferable."

We stroll down the cobblestone path along the canal. I look into the shops and admire the fantastic details of the place. I always thought of Vegas as the city of sin—sex, drugs, and gambling. But now I see the appeal. This place is stunning. I love it here.

"What are the other hotels like?" I ask.

"Oh, they're great. They all have a theme of some sort. It's real fun to visit them all and just walk around. We could do that this weekend. There's one that makes you feel like you're in Paris, and one modeled after

New York City, one is modeled after Rome, another has amazing art. They all kind of bring something special to the table. Oh, we could walk over to the Bellagio fountain. It looks cool at night with different lights."

"That all sounds fun. Yeah, let's visit them all tomorrow."

"Sounds like a plan."

The day has been perfect. I'm not sure if it's the fact that Beckett and I are married or that everything has been wonderful and romantic, but I'm feeling things I shouldn't. I'm so attracted to Beckett right now that I can't stop thinking about what his body would feel like pressed against mine.

*Whoa.*

It's the wine and the walk through Venice. That has to be it.

The fact that Beckett is one of the hottest men I've ever met has nothing to do with the butterflies doing backflips in the pit of my belly. Oddly enough, gorgeous men are usually a turnoff for me and leave a bad taste in my mouth. But unlike most of the attractive men I've had the misfortune of knowing, he's not a total douchebag. He's sincerely good.

This is the first moment I've had any regrets all day. I should have fake married a troll. Beckett is too much temptation, and something about him, here in Sin City, has me all worked up.

"What is it?" Beckett asks.

Walking through the hall of the hotel, we approach our room door.

"Nothing."

Using the key card, he opens the door, and my heart plummets when I step inside. There must be a couple of dozen vases full of lilies that look like the ones in my bouquet placed around every flat surface in the suite. It's too much, too sweet, too thoughtful. I need to go into my room, shut my door, and stay in there until we leave this intoxicating city.

But I don't take my own advice. Instead, I turn to Beckett, my eyes wet with emotion. "What is this?" My voice cracks. "When did you have time to do this?"

"I snapped a picture of your bouquet at the wedding and sent it to the concierge. Told him to order vases of flowers that looked exactly like your wedding bouquet and have them set up in the room before we got back from dinner. I figured you liked the flower since you chose it for our wedding."

"I love them. They're my favorite. They were my mom's favorite. Thank you so much. This is too sweet. You shouldn't be this nice, Beckett."

He laughs. "I can't help it. I like being nice. I like making people happy, and I really love making you happy."

"Thank you." I take a step toward him and wrap my arms around his neck.

He circles his arms around my waist, and I lean into the embrace. Beckett's hard chest presses against me as it rises and falls in labored breaths. He's just as affected as I am. I feel it in the way he holds me. I hear it in his breaths. Most of all, his arousal is evident in the way the bulge beneath his suit pants pushes against my abdomen.

"We can't." My words come out broken.

"I know."

"We shouldn't." I inhale the scent of him. He smells woodsy, spicy, and clean all at once, and the ache between my thighs grows.

"I know," he repeats.

Moving my face away from his chest, I stare into his eyes. His pupils are dilated, and his lips parted. "Maybe we should just call it a night and go to our rooms," I whisper.

"Okay."

I don't move, and neither does he.

"Beckett," I plead, for what I'm not sure.

"Tell me to go, Elena. Tell me to walk away from you, and I will. You hold the power."

I open my mouth to speak, to tell him to go, but I can't form the words. Instead, I shake my head. "I can't."

"What do you want, Elena? Be honest."

"This isn't real, Beckett."

"I know." His voice remains hoarse and husky.

"It's going to end."

"I know that too."

I squeeze my thighs together, needing relief. The desire is painful. "It can't mean anything."

"Okay." Beckett's hold tightens on my back. "We're two consenting adults, Elena. Sex can just be sex. It doesn't have to be a promise of something more. It can just be for fun, to feel good. You know?"

"But we're married. It could muddy the waters."

"If we can't have a little fun during all this, then we're doing something wrong." The corner of his lips tilts up into a sexy smirk, and he tucks a lock of my hair behind my ear.

"Okay."

He shakes his head. "I need to hear you say it."

I swallow. "I want it."

He raises a brow. "What do you want, Elena? You'll have to be more specific."

"I want to have sex for fun and not have it mean anything."

"Okay, then." He chuckles, deep and raspy. "I'll take it."

With that, he crashes his lips to mine.

# CHAPTER
## EIGHTEEN

BECKETT

It's hard to show restraint when you're married to a fucking queen. There is nothing about this woman that I don't find irresistible.

I've known that Elena is attracted to me. I can't say for sure if her attraction is at the same level as mine since I'm flat-out obsessed, but it's clear she wants me.

Now that she's said it out loud…

Fuck me.

My lips move against hers as my tongue requests entrance. A whimper leaves her throat, and she presses her body against mine as our tongues start to caress one another. This woman can kiss. Her mouth alone could get me off. As these thoughts run through my mind, she pulls away. Her lips are swollen, and her eyes wide. Breaths uneven, she drops her stare to the evidence of my arousal and looks up at me in question.

For the walking sex goddess she is, she's timid as hell.

"What do you want, baby? You want to explore?" My voice is gravelly as my need builds.

Her tongue peeks out between her lips, and she nods.

Leaning forward, I kiss up her neck and suck on her earlobe. "You don't have to ask. My body is yours. Take what you want." My lips ghost the shell of her ear.

She moans as I take a step back, allowing the wall to support me. I unbutton my dress shirt and shake both my shirt and jacket off. The articles of clothing fall to the floor, leaving my chest bare. Elena smooths her palms against my pecs. She stares in fascination as her touch grazes my skin. Her hand runs the length of my rib cage, and she moves forward. She circles my nipple with her warm mouth and flicks it with her tongue.

I hiss. The sensation of Elena's mouth on me has my nerve endings on fire.

She glances up through her long black lashes, and her doe eyes look at me in question.

"That feels so good. Your mouth is magic, baby."

Elena's eyes flutter closed, and a whimper escapes her mouth. The praise turns her on. She needs it, the reassurance. We're a match made in heaven because talking is one of my superpowers.

Her movements carry more intention, and she moves down my torso with more confidence. Without hesitation, she unbuckles my leather belt and unfastens my slacks. Her fingers slide into my pants, and she tugs them down to my ankles. My hard length springs free, and Elena studies it. An equally fascinated and heated expression lines her features.

The sight of Elena on her knees wearing the dress we were married in, staring at my dick as if it's the most incredible thing she's seen, is intoxicating as hell. My balls clench, antsy for release.

"Put your sexy mouth on me, baby," I order.

Elena licks her lips. Fisting the base of my dick, she inserts the rest into her mouth. I move my hips forward, hitting the back of her throat.

Releasing a groan, I run my fingers through Elena's hair, fisting my hands against her head, guiding her over my length. She works me in her mouth, sucking and licking to perfection.

"Fuck, Elena. That's so good. You're amazing."

She whimpers and squeezes her thighs together, and fuck if that isn't sexy as hell. Praise and dirty words fall from my lips as Elena works her mouth over me harder and faster. With each word of praise, she gets more worked up until her body trembles. She presses the palm of her hand between her thighs, and the interior of her mouth vibrates from her moans.

Taking hold of her shoulders, I push her mouth off me. I scoop my arms under hers and lift her from the floor. Kicking my pants from my ankles, I lift Elena and carry her to the closest bed.

"It's your turn, baby," I say between kisses and lay her down on the plush bedding. I push her white dress up to her waist. "This stays on for now. I want to see you fall apart wearing the dress you married me in." I remove her lacy thong and toss it to the floor. A hand on each knee, I push her legs to the side, opening her wide for me. "Fuuuck," I groan. My head falls back, and I pull in a deep breath before I return my stare. "You're so sexy. You have no idea how insanely gorgeous you are."

Elena is naked from the waist down. Knees to the side, she's spread open, her core is dripping with desire, and I've never wanted to be somewhere more. The dress pools under her breasts, and her chest is flushed, as is her face. She breathes heavy, her brown eyes scanning my naked body.

I drop to my knees and insert two fingers into her warmth. We release a collective groan as they move in and out. "You're so wet, so ready," I say, removing my fingers. Sliding them north, I circle her bud of swollen nerves before returning them to her entrance. I do this a few times until she's whimpering. She presses her cheek against the bed, her eyes closed tight as I make her feel good. "I want to taste you when you come for me. Are you going to be a good girl and come for me, baby?"

Face still tight with pleasure, she nods.

"Good." I push my two fingers inside her and, this time, let them work against her front wall as I circle her clit with my mouth. I finger her entrance and suck and lick her bundle of nerves until she's writhing.

"Beckett!" she whimpers.

She's so close. I can feel her internal walls starting to spasm around my fingers as her breathing becomes full-on moans. I continue the assault until she's screaming, her body trembling as she falls over the edge to ecstasy.

Fuck me if Elena coming isn't the hottest sight I've ever seen. Everything about this woman fascinates me.

Sated and boneless, she comes down from her high as I retrieve a condom from my bag.

Condom on, I stand over her, breathing heavily. "You ready?"

She nods.

A grin finds my face. "You know I need the words, baby. What do you want, Elena?"

Sitting up, she pulls her dress over her head and discards it. She unclips her bra and drops it on the floor as well. She looks up at me, her eyes challenging. "I need you to fuck me, Beckett. I want you to make me feel amazing."

"Oh, I can do that, baby." I grin.

Climbing atop her naked body, I cage her head in with my arms and kiss her senseless. We both know this is just about sex and feeling good, but I can't deny the part of me that wants it all with this woman.

I position myself at her entrance and push inside. Her eyes close, and she moans. "Fuck yeah, I knew you'd be a perfect fit." I pick up the pace, thrusting in deeper.

Lifting one of her legs, I push it up and to the side, holding the leg with my arm. Opening her wider, I'm able to go deeper. The pleasure dials up a notch as we both cry out in pleasure. "You feel so good. I knew you'd feel so good."

My words cause her to whimper. She reaches out and threads her fingers through my hair, pulling my face toward hers. We kiss. My tongue enters her mouth and mirrors the movements my body makes down below. Elena moans into my mouth with each thrust. The connection is unreal, so completely satisfying that I struggle to hold off my orgasm. I want to give her as much of me as I can.

We're a mess of skin, sweat, moans, and sensations as our bodies come together over and over again. This feels so much deeper than a quick fuck or a one-night stand. It's unlike anything I've felt before. If I were being honest with myself, that thought would give me pause. But I choose to ignore it and simply feel all the pleasure her body gives me.

Her fingertips dig into my scalp, and she holds my face closer. Her kisses become desperate as she chases her release. She cries out, her body trembling as I pound harder into her. Reaching a hand between our slick bodies, I find her clit and squeeze it between my thumb and forefinger. She moans as her body convulses beneath me. I let go, and my orgasm rips through my body as we fall into ecstasy together.

I roll off her, and we lie side by side, catching our breaths.

"I don't know about you, but Vegas just became my favorite place," I say.

Elena chuckles. "Yeah, it does not disappoint."

Rolling over on my side, I prop my head up. "You're so beautiful."

Elena rolls her eyes. "Stop. You can't be all mushy and sweet."

"Why not?"

"Because it will confuse things."

I furrow my brows. "There are two people in this room, and neither one of us is confused. I can think you're beautiful, a walking sex goddess, love everything about your body including being inside it, and not be confused as to what this arrangement is."

She scoffs. "I am definitely not a walking sex goddess."

"Oh yes, you are. You're amazing. I can't ever remember coming that hard."

Her chest rises, and she bites her bottom lip. I don't miss the way her nipples harden, and I'm astounded by how easily my words affect her. If she lets us, we can have a lot of fun.

This has been one of the best days of my life.

I've fucked a lot of people, but I've never fucked my wife, and I have to say, hands down—amazing. Ten out of ten. Highly recommend.

# CHAPTER
## NINETEEN

ELENA

Beckett stands over the room service cart, picks a piece of bacon up from a plate, and plops it in his mouth. He's wearing nothing but form-fitting gray boxer briefs, and even though I've just woken up, I'm having a hard time focusing on anything other than him.

"I didn't know what you wanted, so I ordered one of everything on the breakfast menu," he says. He lifts silver domes off each plate. "There are crepes, eggs, waffles, pancakes, sausage, bacon, oatmeal, fruit, toast. I mean, anything you want, really. If you're craving something that's not here, let me know. I'll get it for you."

I stretch my arms over my head and suppress a chuckle. "I think the food you ordered will do just fine." I notice the silk robe Beckett has draped over the bedside table for me, and my heart twists at how thoughtful he is. I work my naked body out from beneath the sheet and quickly cover up with the robe. "I'll be right back," I say before hurrying to the bathroom.

The bathroom in this suite is bigger than the living room and kitchen combined in my old apartment. Beckett didn't spare any expenses this weekend, that's for sure. He's made it so special from the moment I stepped out of his condo to see the limo. Not many people can say they've been through a Starbucks drive-through in a limousine.

I use the restroom and brush my teeth. Toothbrush in my mouth, I stretch my muscles. I'm abnormally sore this morning. Every inch of my body aches. Granted, I used muscles last night that I haven't used in years.

Sex with Beckett is incredible. I can't blame him for being a self-proclaimed slut. If I had that kind of skill in bed, I'd probably be a slut, too. The guy can move and kiss and lick…

My core starts to warm, and I shake my head. *Nope. Calm down.*

I can't go there again today. Can I?

While sweet, this whole weekend is so confusing. It would've been in our best interests to have signed the marriage certificate at the courthouse, as I had planned, and called it a day. Kept everything platonic. Things were working. Yes, everything Beckett has planned for our Vegas wedding getaway has been amazing, but a fake wedding doesn't need to be incredible. It's not the most important day of our lives.

And now that I've had his magical dick inside me, it's opened a whole other can of worms. Just thinking about the way my body reacts to both his words and his touch has me aching to feel him again.

I agree that we're adults and can have casual sex if we want, but it doesn't feel casual with Beckett. It's far too good to be classified as such. We live, work, eat dinners, and binge shows together—if we add in sex, we might as well be a real married couple. And that's not what either of us wants. There has to be a line.

I spit and wash out my mouth with water. Pulling in a breath, I steady my resolve. Today will be sightseeing as we had planned and nothing more. Last night was fun, but a repeat is too risky. It's settled, then.

Exiting the bathroom, I rejoin Beckett.

"There's my beautiful wife." Beckett grins and extends a mug to me. "Coffee?"

"Yes, please." I look at the amazing spread of food. "This looks delicious."

"Well, eat up."

Taking a couple of plates of food, I join Beckett at the table. He isn't acting any differently than he usually does, but everything feels strange. The air between us is heavy and awkward, at least for me. This man, my friend, co-worker, and accomplice in my scheme, had his face between my legs three times last night and his dick inside me five. And now, he's stuffing a pancake in his mouth and talking about the Vegas show options like we didn't have sex to the point of utter exhaustion last night.

In fact, my ass cheeks were on this table as he ate me out at one point in the night. I sucked his dick against that wall. We did it on the bed, in the shower, and everywhere between. It was a lust-filled night of insanity, and now we're sitting across from one another casually having breakfast like none of that happened.

"Is the sausage spicy?"

I swallow the sausage and egg in my mouth. "What?"

With his fork, he points at the sausage on my plate. "Is the sausage too spicy? Your chest is all red."

Dropping my gaze to my flushed skin, I tighten my robe. "No, it's fine."

His lips tilt up into a smirk, and he quirks a brow. "What were you thinking about?"

"Nothing." I shake my head. "Shows and whatever else you were talking about."

He chuckles. "You're lying."

"I am not!" I protest. "I wasn't thinking about anything."

He shovels another fork full of pancakes into his mouth and shakes his head. "Don't worry. I've been thinking about it, too."

I take another bite of my cheesy omelet and shrug. "I'm not sure what you're referring to." Though I've lived four decades, I've never acquired the skills that would allow me to talk about casual sex as if it's no big deal.

It's a big deal to me as I haven't had much of it. As my adult years passed and my time was focused on Ari and school, sex wasn't an option. I didn't have time to date, casually or otherwise. Though I'm more mature than Beckett in many ways, this is not one of them. I feel like a twelve-year-old girl saying the word penis out loud for the first time. My inexperience is embarrassing.

Beckett laughs. "Really? Well, I can recount the events of last night in graphic detail if you'd like. I remember every taste, smell, feeling, and sound." His voice lowers, causing my heart to race.

"No!" I hold out my hand. "That won't be necessary."

He puckers his lips, squinting his eyes. "So you remember? It's all coming back to you now?"

I roll my eyes. "Yes, I remember."

"And?"

"And what?" I drop my fork on my plate. "What do you want me to say, Beckett?"

He shrugs. "I don't know. You were obviously thinking about it, so I was curious as to what parts you were thinking about. Was it good for you?"

I scoff and pin him with a stare. "If you remember every detail, you obviously know it was."

"Yeah, I know." He smiles. "I just really get off on hearing you say it."

I shake my head. "Well, there will be no getting off today. That was a wedding night-only special, and its time limit has expired. Today, we are going back to platonic married friends."

"Really?" He stands from the table and returns his plates to the room service cart.

His tone makes my core clench with need. He removes my plates and cup of coffee and orders me to stand. My brain tells me not to, but my body jumps at the chance to comply.

He stands behind me and kisses my neck as he unties my robe. The silky fabric falls to my feet, leaving me naked. My chest rises and falls, and my heart thumps wildly in my chest as he runs his palms down my arms, leaving goose bumps in their wake. He slides my hair over my shoulder so it falls over my chest and proceeds to pepper soft kisses across my back, working his lips from my shoulder blades down to the crack of my ass and back up again.

His back to my front, he leans in and pulls my earlobe into his mouth as his hands circle. He rolls my hardened nipples between his thumb and forefinger. "Does that feel good?" he whispers against the sensitive skin beneath my ear.

"Yes." The word comes out as a moan, and I realize I'm powerless to resist him. I want him more than I've ever wanted anyone. The relationship may not be real, but nothing about the way he makes my body feel is fake.

"Tell me what you were thinking about? What parts made you feel good?" He lowers his hand from my breast until he's between my thighs, rubbing my clit.

"All of it. I loved all of it," I pant as he works his fingers over my most sensitive part.

"I loved all of it, too," he whispers against my ear. His hot breath mixed with his movements below are working me into a frenzy. "I love the way you taste. I love how responsive you are to my words. I love to hear your sounds of pleasure. I love the way my dick felt in your mouth and in your pussy. I love how well we fit together. I love how hard I come when I'm with you."

His fingers rub faster, and I lean my head back. Turning my face to the side, I wrap my arm around his head and pull him toward me. I moan as his tongue enters my mouth. He kisses me senseless as his fingers push my body to the edge. The orgasm hits, and I cry into his mouth as waves of euphoria course through me.

At this moment, I know we're not leaving this suite for the rest of the weekend. There's not a show, casino, or sight in this entire state that could top the experience of having sex with Beckett. It's beyond addicting, and as I come down from my high, I'm already looking forward to my next one.

I step away from Beckett, bend at the waist, and allow my top half to press against the table. A condom wrapper rips open behind me, and a moment later, Beckett's at my entrance.

"Beckett?"

"What is it, baby?"

"This has to stay here. Us, this way, doesn't leave Vegas. Okay?"

He slides into me with a satisfied groan. "Whatever you want."

Arms stretched out, my fingers curl around the edge of the table as Beckett pushes into me. He holds my hips and thrusts into me again and again. We both vocalize our pleasure. We haven't even finished breakfast, and I'm almost two orgasms in.

Yeah, the only sight I want to see this wedding weekend is Beckett's naked body, and I have no doubt he'll be more than happy to comply.

# CHAPTER
## TWENTY

BECKETT

*What happens in Vegas stays in Vegas.*

That expression has always been comical to me because of the over-sharer I am. Nothing that happens anywhere stays a secret for long.

However, Elena is taking the expression at face value.

Things have gone back to the way we were since getting home. We're comfortable roommates—hanging out and watching TV and having dinner together every night. She sleeps in her room and I in mine. We drive separately to work every day "in case one of us needs to run errands after PT." Elena is so worried about these possible errands, yet we've been home for a week, and today is the first time she's gone anywhere after work.

I get it, I suppose. There have to be some boundaries, or things are bound to get messy. However, the way I see it, if you're going to have a live-in spouse, why not enjoy all the benefits? I'm capable of being intimate with someone without feelings getting involved. Maybe she isn't, and she's insisting on a platonic relationship to make things easier for her. If that's the case, I can respect it, but I don't like it.

But I miss the uninhibited, carefree, fun—and fine, I'll admit—naked Elena. Vegas weekend was the best weekend I've had in a long time. We didn't leave our hotel suite once after our wedding night. We ordered room service and spent the entirety of our stay in, pleasing one another. Elena is the most gorgeous woman I've seen, but Elena in bed is smoking hot. Nothing is sexier than a woman breaking free of her inhibitions and fully committing to the moment. I've had a lot of hot sex in my life, but nothing compares to our wedding weekend. Elena is going to make some man very lucky someday.

I don't know, maybe she's right. Definite feelings are involved. How can there not be? I miss sleeping with her at night, like actually sleeping. My king-sized bed is suddenly too big for me to sleep alone. I need Elena's soft skin up against me. I miss the intimacy and the connection we shared. I realize I shouldn't, but now that I've had her, it's hard to be without.

I've finished loading the dishwasher and am closing it as the door to our condo bursts open. It's quickly closed, and Elena comes running into the kitchen with a broad smile on her face.

"What is it?" Amusement lines my voice, and I find the way Elena beams with excitement completely adorable.

"Today is a good day, husband." She raises her eyebrows. She only uses the descriptor when she's in a playful mood, and admittedly, I love it. Something about the word falling from her lips drives me crazy in the best way possible.

"Oh yeah?" I chuckle. "Why is that, wife?"

She takes my hand and leads me to the living room. "Sit," she orders.

I plop my ass onto the couch cushion. Leaning back, I get comfortable as she paces before me.

She talks adamantly, moving her hands about. "Well, after work, I drove to my father's."

"You did? Why didn't you tell me? I would've gone with you."

She gives me a warm smile. "I know, and I appreciate it, but I wanted to talk to him on my own. I felt it was important that I arrive alone, stand up for myself, and prove that I'm capable of inheriting his fortune."

"Okay."

"So I did. First." She raises a finger. "I showed up without an appointment or notifying his lawyers. You're right, I shouldn't need to schedule an appointment to see my father through two stuffy old men, so I didn't. I just showed up. He was there, of course, because he has little strength to do anything else. I handed him our marriage license, and he called his lawyers."

She continues. "While we waited for his legal team to arrive, I talked, and he had no choice but to listen. I went over everything I've done and accomplished in the past twenty years. I told him about Ariana and the perfect human she's turned out to be. I voiced my regrets that my relationship with him had to be the way it was. I let it be known that I would've loved to have him in my life if he would've just accepted me for me."

"Really?"

"Yeah." She nods. "He didn't say much, but I expected that. He's too proud and stubborn to admit he was wrong, and I knew he'd never take any blame, apologize, or voice regrets, and he didn't. But he heard me. He understands where I stand and what I feel. He knows he hurt me and that he missed out on a relationship with his amazing granddaughter. I mean, nothing I said changes anything, but I needed to say it."

"Okay, good." The corner of my mouth tilts into a grin, and I'm filled with pride. She faced her fears, and she's better for it.

"Yeah, it was good. Then the lawyers came and had all the new paperwork ready. It's all laid out. Every-thing—every business, asset, and cent—goes to me. And I'm sorry to tell you, but he had it written in there that if you and I were to get a divorce after his death, you don't get a penny from his estate."

"Oh, bummer. Well, that sucks... you know I'm only doing this for your money."

She laughs. "I know. Sucks for you, but anyway, it is what it is."

Standing from the couch, I walk over to her and hug her. "That's all good news."

"Yeah, it is, but there's more." She puckers her lip in a smirk.

"More?" I take a step back. "Do tell."

"Well…" She steeples her hands in front of her face. "I got the MRI results back from your test yesterday, and based on the results and your performance in PT, you're cleared to start full-day practices with the team!"

"Fuck yeah!" I pick her up and spin her around. "That's better than any fortune."

The team's lower-intensity training months are over, and come Monday, we're back to full days of practice, skills, and lifting to prepare for the start of the season. I wasn't sure I'd be ready to go back, so I'm beyond relieved that I am.

I set Elena down. "I knew you'd be thrilled. I'm excited to start working with some of your teammates. The only one I really know is you."

"First, I'm the only one you need to know." I pin her with a stare, causing her to giggle. "Second, you only work with injured guys, so let's hope you don't get to know any of them because we have a Cup to win this season."

"I know. Of course I'm not hoping for serious injuries. I can guide players to make healthy choices and in the development of practices that will keep their bodies in top shape. That's what I meant. Anyway, this is the best day, and we should celebrate."

"Agreed. What did you have in mind?"

The air in the room changes. It grows heavy, stuffy with desire. I feel it, and there's no doubt she does, too.

She swallows hard and takes another step back from me, putting distance between us. She runs her hands up and down her arms. "Um... I don't know. We could go out to eat or something? Maybe see a movie?"

I suppress a chuckle. Is she serious with this *see a movie* shit? She knows exactly what she wants. The need is pulsating from her body. It's visceral, weighing heavily on us both.

The way I see it, this could play out one of two ways. I can play nice, go along with her charade, and look up movie times, or I could cut through the bullshit and take what I want. This week has been way too lonely without her, making my choice clear.

Besides, I can't remember a time I haven't gone after what I want, and I'm not about to start now.

In three quick steps, I close the gap between us. Threading my fingers through her hair, I pull her face toward mine and kiss her—hard and unrelenting, exactly how I've wanted to for a week now. My lips have craved hers. I've missed her touch, her moans of pleasure, her body, and her soul. She's given me a fraction of herself this past week, the "forced smile-everything is fine" version. I can't survive on that, not when I know what the real Elena is like, the woman I got to have in Vegas.

She pulls her mouth from mine. "Beck, we can't." Her words hold no conviction.

"Why not?" Hands against her head, I keep her face close to mine.

"Because it's not real. We have to... have boundaries."

My tongue sweeps out to wet my lips. "We've been over this. We're consenting adults, Elena. There is nothing wrong with enjoying the perks of this arrangement. There's no deceit here. We know where this is going and where it's not. No one is taking advantage of anyone else."

She breathes heavy. Pupils dilated, she holds me in her stare but doesn't respond.

"Tell me you don't want to feel me inside you, Elena. Tell me you don't want me to make your body writhe with pleasure. Just say the word, and this will be over. I'll look up movie times. Say it."

She bites her bottom lip and gives me a slight shake of her head. "I can't."

"Tell me what you want," I order, done with being the one always chasing her. Her desire is equal to my own, and she needs to own it.

She remains quiet.

I drop my hands and take a step back.

"Wait," she calls out. "I want you. I want you to fuck me. Is that what you want to hear?" Her words sound angry, but I know it's the lust that weighs heavy on us both that makes her sound that way.

I smile. "That's exactly what I want to hear. Take off your clothes." We make quick work of disrobing. In a matter of seconds, we stand naked before each other. I nod toward the sofa. "Turn around. Bend over. I'm going to take you hard and fast."

Elena whimpers, her mouth falls agape at my words. She hurries toward the sofa and does as instructed. I snatch a condom from the drawer of the coffee table and slide it over my length.

The sight of Elena bent over the sofa, her ass on full display, her body shaking in anticipation of my touch is a fucking dream.

"Good girl." Standing behind her, I glide my fingers from her neck, down her spine, and to her plump ass cheeks. "You have the best ass." I squeeze her flesh, and she releases a heated sigh. "Open up for me, baby."

Elena steps to the side, and I slide two fingers into her opening. She's warm, wet, and ready. I release a hiss of pleasure, and my dick throbs with need. "You're always so ready for me." Removing my fingers, I bend my knees and position the tip of my dick at her opening. I tease her entrance, and she cries out, desperate. I grab her hips and pull her onto my length. We release a collective moan of pleasure. I start moving, slamming my body into hers, going as deep as I can. I thrust my hips and pull her back, hitting her deep inside. She asked me to fuck her, and as the people pleaser I am, I comply with full force.

Her lust-filled screams fill the space, and I pound into her again and again. My balls tingle as pleasure travels through my body, lighting up every nerve. "Touch yourself," I huff out between labored breaths. "Come with me."

She steadies herself with one arm while the other dips between her legs. In a matter of seconds, she's shaking and screaming my name. Hearing my name fall from her lips amid her pleasure-laden cries pushes me over the edge. My fingers dig into her skin, and I thrust inside her quivering walls as we fall over the edge together.

Completely sated, I pull out of her and discard the condom. We fall onto the sofa. I pull her boneless body on top of me, feeling the rise and fall of her chest as she catches her breath. I just had her, yet it's not enough. I need her again. Dipping my face, I pull her nipple into my mouth and suck.

"Beck." Elena whimpers. "I need a minute."

"And I need you." I lick the skin of her breast, slick with sweat. I can't help myself. When I have Elena this way, I become obsessed. She's my drug, and no matter how many times I have it, I'll always chase the high.

"This… is why… I suggested… boundaries." She moans as I flick her nipple with my tongue.

"And this glorious feeling…" I squeeze her ass before sliding my hands up her body and into her hair. I press my mouth to hers and pull her bottom lip between my teeth. "Is why I say fuck 'em."

She pushes off me and sits to my side on the sofa. She drapes her legs over my thighs. "Beckett, I'm serious. We need to talk about this."

"Sure, whatever you want." I twist her nipple between my thumb and forefinger.

She slaps my hand away. "Stop. This is serious, Beckett. I can't focus when you're touching me."

I raise my hands in mock surrender. "Okay. Talk."

"Well, admittedly, I haven't had much sex in my life, but I feel like our chemistry is off the charts, at least it is for me."

"Oh, it's definitely off the charts, Elena."

She chews on the side of her cheek and looks across the room before returning her gaze to me. "Okay, so… don't you think it will be harder to stop when this is all over? We have to be careful not to let feelings get involved."

"No feelings. Just sex. We've discussed this."

"I know, I'm just nervous."

I quirk a brow. "That I'm going to fall madly in love with you and not be able to let you go in a couple of months when your dad is gone?"

"Exactly."

"You don't have to worry about that. It's not going to happen. Unless you think you're going to fall for me?"

"No," she barks out. "I'm not going to fall for you. This is only temporary."

I shrug. "Okay then, we have no problem. Let's just have fun. It'd be a shame for two people who fit so perfectly together not to." I wag my brows with a smirk, causing Elena to laugh.

"Okay. You're right. As long as you're sure it won't be an issue."

I slide my hand up her thigh. "Oh, I'm sure." My hand dips down between her thighs, and she spreads her legs, inviting me in. I push my fingers into her opening, and her head falls back as she releases an audible sigh. "I think we have some more celebrating to do. Wanna take this to the bedroom?"

"Definitely," she says.

That's all the invitation I need.

# CHAPTER
## TWENTY-ONE

ELENA

"You know, it's not good form to arrive at a wedding looking better than the bride." Beckett moves my hair to the side and presses his lips against my shoulder.

I playfully swat him away. "I will not look better than the bride. Your sister will be stunning."

"Yeah, she will. She always is."

I run my fingers through my curled locks to break up the strands and give more of a beach wave look. "Your family sure has great genes."

He stands behind me, looking dapper in his suit, and circles his arms around my waist. He stares into the mirror, his reflection supplying me with his classic smirk. "Are you saying I'm hot?"

"Stop digging for compliments." I attempt to remove his hands from my middle so I can finish getting ready. "Let go. I need to finish my makeup."

"Answer the question."

With a roll of my eyes, I say, "Yes, Beckett… you are hot. Now move."

Releasing his hold on me, he takes a step back. "It wouldn't hurt if you acknowledged my rugged, handsome good looks a little more often, you know?"

"You're ridiculous." I chuckle. "And if you don't let me finish my makeup, we're going to be late."

He raises his hands, palms out. "Fine. Go ahead. I'll leave you alone." He takes a seat on the bed and watches me.

An amused sigh escapes. "You are way too clingy, Mr. Feldmore."

"I can't help it. You're too beautiful."

"Anyway." I ignore his compliment. "Are you sure I should be going to this? You can say I'm sick. I feel weird going to such an important event in your family's life."

"Of course you should go. The whole team is invited. You'd be there anyway."

"Yeah, but not as your wife. I don't think your family has opened up to the idea, not that I can blame them." I swipe the bronzing brush over my cheeks.

"It's fine. Don't worry so much. You're the team

doctor. You need to be there. Plus, I want you there with me."

I apply lip gloss and slide into my heels. "Okay, let's do this."

Iris and Cade's wedding is being held in her parents' backyard. The stunning house sits on beautiful grounds. It's about as fancy of a home as one could have before it'd be considered gaudy and pretentious like the one I grew up in. Beckett tells me that Iris planned every detail of the wedding, and while they could've gotten married anywhere, they chose this backyard wedding so it didn't interrupt the guys' training schedule.

But this is no ordinary backyard wedding. The space has been transformed into an elegant, whimsical place full of pink flowers and twinkling lights. I've only seen locations this beautiful on Pinterest, for the ten minutes I thought I had time to be crafty several years ago.

Iris walks down the aisle on the arm of her father. She looks stunning and so very happy. The Cranes players wait at the end of the aisle, half on Cade's side and the other half on Iris's. There isn't a bridesmaid in sight, just a sea of handsome men in suits. It's quite sweet, really—a visual representation of how close this team is and how much Iris and Cade mean to them all.

The sight brings a pang of sadness because I can't help thinking about the wedding Beckett and I shared, just the two of us—none of his friends. If we'd gotten married for real, I imagine the event would look similar to this. There's no question he's the heart of the team. And while he may get his team-filled wedding someday, it will always be his second. I carry the guilt of tainting this future experience for him. He's reassured me many times that he doesn't see it that way, but that's only because he would never say anything to make me feel bad. But the fact remains.

I have to remain focused on all the good I'll do with the money. It's the only thing that keeps me from drowning in guilt for my actions and all the lies.

The ceremony wraps up, and Beckett hurries over. Grabbing my hands in his, he leans in for a kiss. "You doing okay?"

"Great."

"Awesome. So a few magazines are here for pictures. I'm going to oversee that ordeal and kick 'em out when they've overstayed their welcome. It shouldn't take too long."

A smile tugs at my lips. "You need to stop worrying about me. I'm a grown woman, Beck. I can handle myself for a few minutes." I smooth my hands along the sleeves of his suit jacket.

He supplies another kiss. It's short and sweet, and despite my earlier declaration, it brings a calmness to me. "I'm not saying you can't handle yourself. I'm just giving you an update on where I'll be. Have you ever thought that I'm the one who can't wait to get back to you?"

"Uh-huh." I fuss with his tie, which is perfect as is, but it gives me a reason to touch him. "So that's how it is?"

He grins. "You know I'm obsessed." He nods toward the tent with the tables of food. "Go hang out with the guys. They'll make the time go faster."

"For you?"

"Exactly. If I know you're not lonely, the time will go faster *for me*, and the sooner I'll be at your side."

My hands run down his chest, stopping on his abs. His six-pack is hidden beneath an undershirt, dress shirt, and suit jacket, but I swear I can feel them. Perhaps I've felt his abdomen muscles so often as of late, my imagination is running wild. "You're awfully clingy. You need to work on that before…" Beckett's face falls, and I don't finish the thought. My intention was a light-hearted, playful moment, but mentioning the future tends to put an immediate damper on the situation.

*Before this is over.*

*Before I move out.*

*Before I leave.*

Regardless of how I finish that sentence, it wouldn't have been well received. And I know that is a problem in itself, one that I ignore because life is really good right now, and I'm choosing to relish in it as long as I can.

Beckett quickly recovers, and his charming smile resurfaces. "I won't be long." He kisses me again before turning to leave. With a sigh, I watch as he walks over to a beautiful pink rose canopy where Iris and Cade pose for cameras.

Taking his advice, I make my way to the food tent.

"Doc!" A round of cheers explodes when I enter, and I can't help the smile that crosses my face.

These guys have been wonderful, and I've enjoyed working with them over the past few months. They've all made an effort to get to know me—not because I'm technically Beckett's wife but because I'm part of the Cranes. Beckett's always said they're his family, and I see that now. Shame over my initial feelings on this job is my daily companion. I'm embarrassed I was so quick to judge them, so sure they'd be like the excuse for men I've known in the past. The past four months have been a vivid realization of how badly my past tainted my view of the world. I've changed so much over the past several months, and I can't deny that Beckett has been the catalyst for my transformation.

Max and Jaden, the team's starting defenders, hold up pink heart-shaped cookies and laugh.

"What'd I miss?" I ask.

Max hands me the cookie. In frosting, it reads, "*A heartbreaker no more.*"

I stare at the cookie in my hand. "What does it mean?"

The guys tell me about their team tradition of handing out nicknames, and how Cade got his.

"You see," Bash says, "Iris thinks that a cookie is going to put an end to a nickname as if it ever would." He laughs.

I look around at the group of men surrounding me. "Do you all have names? And how do you get them?"

"Most of the guys do. They just kind of come on naturally. Sometimes it takes years to spark a name. Other times, the player earns one right off the bat like Feltmore." Jaden raises a brow.

With a roll of my eyes, I scoff. "I'm very aware of Beckett's nickname. So are you telling me that name is here to stay?"

"Hell yeah, it's here to stay," Bash teases. "It's a good one, too. It took me two years to get my name. The guys starting calling me Cookie Monster after our bye week vacation in Barbados when I won the choco-late chip cookie baking competition."

"Cookie Monster is quite tough," I kid with a chuckle.

"When you taste his cookies, you'll understand. They're lethally good," Jaden says.

"I can't say I've had a cookie taste so good it's deadly."

"Then you haven't had mine." Bash smirks.

"So what are the other nicknames?" I question.

Max answers, "Well, our beast of a goalie, Gunner Dreven, is fittingly enough called The Beast."

"Makes sense." I nod.

He continues, "I'm TJ Maxx." I cover my mouth in an attempt not to laugh, and Max rolls his eyes. "You can laugh. It's dumb as fuck."

I school my features. "So why TJ Maxx?"

"I had a very short"—he glares toward the guys—"run of wearing knockoff brand name clothing. I was young. It was my first year on the team. I wasn't starting or making a shit ton of money then. So I figured why not save some money on my clothes."

Jaden howls in laughter. "Yeah, tell her what that tag said."

Max rolls his eyes and sighs. "I may have had a shirt once with a tag that said Tommy Hulfinger."

I press my lips in a line, but the chuckle escapes.

"Wow. That's bad. Honestly, you're lucky they aren't calling you Hulfinger."

Bash answers. "It was an option."

"What do you know?" Max grumbles. "You weren't even on the team then."

"I've heard the stories. They're classics. I believe there was a rip-off Polo shirt with a donkey?" Bash raises his eyebrows.

"No!" Max holds up his finger, pointing it toward the guys. "It was a horse. It was not a donkey."

"That shit was a fucking donkey, TJ," Gunner's deep voice says as he walks up beside me, joining the group.

Max groans. "I thrift shop once in my life, and it's held over my head forever."

Gunner huffs and passes on by, heading to the bar. He's been nothing but nice to me, but I don't get the feeling he's a super chatty guy.

"Hey." I squeeze Max's arm. "I've been a bargain shopper all my life. There is nothing wrong with finding deals on clothes. Wearing brand names doesn't make anyone better than anyone else."

"However," Jaden says, "there is a difference between saving money and being an idiot. Would you ever wear a T-shirt with a red, white, and blue flag that is ironed onto the shirt on an angle with the words Tommy Hulfinger on the bottom in big, bright letters?

I look at Max with an apologetic expression. "Well, no. Sorry."

The group of guys explodes into laughter, and Max shakes his head.

"What's yours?" I ask Jaden.

"J-Man. Beckett called me that in practice one day, and it stuck. It's not the best, but I'll take it."

I narrow my stare. "Does everyone get one?"

"As in, are you going to get one?" Bash tilts his head, giving me a smug smile. He continues without waiting for my answer. "We've already been playing around with one for you."

"You have?" I raise my brows, anxiety building in my chest. "Do I even want to hear it?"

"Doc Hottie. We used to have Hootie, and it seems like an easy transition," Max says.

"No!" I gasp. "Absolutely not. You guys cannot call me that. That's not professional."

Bash laughs. "And Cookie Monster is? Face it— Hottie is probably going to stick."

"No. I'm serious." I give a little stomp of my heel like a five-year-old throwing a tantrum, but I don't care. I did not struggle through twenty years of school to be called hot.

"I told you guys that name wasn't going to fly." Beckett joins us and circles his arms around my waist.

Jaden scoffs. "You don't have a say in your nickname. It just happens, and there's nothing you can do about it."

My eyes open wide. "Oh, I can do stuff about it." I point my finger around the circle. "I can bench every single one of you that uses that name. I'm serious."

Apparently, my outburst is comical because they all laugh again.

"Come on." Beckett pulls on my hand. "I want to dance with my wife."

He leads me away from the group. "Beck, do not let that be my nickname. I'd rather they call me Dr. Troll-face. Being referred to as hot negates all the hard work I've put in." My voice gets increasingly more squeaky with each word.

Beckett chuckles. "You do not want to be called Trollface, I guarantee it."

"It'd be better than Hottie."

He shrugs. "Okay, I'll try to get it changed to Trollface."

I hit his chest. "This is not a joke, Beckett."

"I know." He wraps his arms around my waist, pulls me against his chest, and we sway to the music. "I'll do what I can. Okay?"

"Please do," I snap.

"Come on, Hottie. Let it go and just dance with me."

"Beckett." I pin him with a warning stare.

He kisses my forehead. "I'm sorry. I really will work on it. But for now, can we just enjoy the reception?"

I nod and blow out a frustrated breath. "Yes, let's enjoy your sister's wedding."

"Good. Now give me a kiss." He puckers his lips, causing me to grin. I hesitate, and he says, "Come on. People are watching. It's all part of the charade. Yes?" He winks. "Now kiss me."

"I guess. If I must."

I press my lips to Beckett's, and the frustration over a silly nickname leaves my body. I'm instantly lost in this kiss, like I am every time his lips touch mine. As I've already discovered, Beckett's lips are magical, and I'm afraid I'll forever be powerless to resist them.

He makes me feel cherished, loved, and protected, and when we're together, it doesn't feel temporary. In fact, it never has. It feels like forever, and that has me more than a little freaked out.

ELENA

"Don't worry. There will be others," I say to Ari over the phone. She had planned to make it home for the Cranes season opener and first home game but has a term paper to work on.

"I feel horrible. This is your first big job, and I want to support you and your team..." There's a pause before she continues, "And your husband."

I hate the fact that she's still so uncomfortable with my marriage to Beckett, but even though I know it shouldn't be, her disdain is amusing. I stifle a laugh. "It's fine. Really. School is your number one priority now. I'll tell Beckett you wished him luck."

"Uh, okay," she grumbles.

"Good luck on your paper. I love you."

"I love you, too. I'm proud of you, Ma."

"Thanks, baby. I'm proud of you, too."

The call ends, and I slide my phone into my back pocket. From a few rows up in the stands, I observe the guys warming up below. We've had some minor sprains and muscle tears in recent weeks, and I'm looking for signs that the injuries haven't healed. The guys tell me they feel great, but I know they'd say anything to be on the ice for the season's first game. Everyone seems to be moving with ease, and they all passed my assessment, so I'm choosing to believe they're all as healthy as they claim.

Beckett flies across the ice and hits the puck with a half-slap shot to his best friend, Cade. The smile on Beckett's face is contagious, and I find my lips curving up. His joy can be felt from here. My chest fills with extreme contentment, and this feeling right here is what led me to sports medicine. The passion that athletes feel toward their sport and the enthusiasm they generate when they're healed enough to play is a fulfilling thing to be a part of.

"They're fun to watch, aren't they?" Iris, Beckett's sister and Cade's wife, stands at my side. I'm not sure when she arrived, but her question startled me.

"Yeah, they are."

"They've been playing together since they were ten with as much joy as they have now."

I grin. "I guess they're in the right profession then. How many people can say they have that much fun at work?"

"Right?" Iris chuckles. "Definitely." She pauses a moment and clears her throat. "Look, I feel like as my brother's wife, I should know you more than I do, and I'm sorry that I haven't made more of an effort."

The truth is, it's not her fault. Beckett and I haven't been very social this summer. We spent the months of August and September wrapped up in each other. Our obsession with one another borders on unhealthy, especially for two people planning to break up soon.

After we returned from Vegas and Beckett convinced me to enjoy the perks of married life, there has been no turning back. We have more sex than is normal. But it makes sense. Beckett is used to a lot of sex, and I'm making up for lost time. I have two decades of orgasms to make up for, and my faux husband is more than happy to oblige.

In the four months I've known Beckett, he's become my best friend. When we get home from work, we eat dinner together, talk, laugh, watch TV, have sex, shower together, have some more sex, and fall asleep in one another's arms. It's a comfortable rhythm that I'll miss when it's gone.

I haven't had the desire to get to know Beckett's friends or family because I'm hoping the deceit will hurt less if they don't know me or love me. We made a choice to lie to our families to secure our secret and, by extension, my inheritance, but it still doesn't feel good.

I shake my head. "No, it's my fault. We've just been so busy and trapped in our own little world."

"Yeah, I've noticed." Iris shoots me a knowing grin. "You two must be enjoying married life. Although I haven't seen much of Beckett lately, he looks happier than ever when I do see him."

"Really?"

"Oh, yeah." She bobs her head. "I mean, he's always been a happy guy, but now, he radiates joy. You know, I admit that I really didn't understand the pairing or the suddenness of it all, but I love my brother, and all I've ever wanted for him is happiness. I guess once he found his person, he didn't want to wait."

"Yeah." I force a smile.

She clears her throat. "Anyway, we should go out sometime for dinner, drinks, whatever. You, me, and the boys."

"That sounds great. We'll have to do that." I look down at her number ten jersey.

She notices my stare. "Are you going to change into your number eighteen jersey?"

"No. I'm here for work, not as Beckett's wife. I'd feel awkward wearing it."

She grins. "I get it. Well, I'm going to finalize some things for the press conference after the game. Enjoy your first Cranes game. They're pretty fun."

"I will. Thanks, Iris."

Returning my attention to the ice, I catch Beckett staring up at me. He gives me a wave and his beautiful smile. I wave back. Blowing out a breath, I turn away from the ice and retreat to my office.

The Cranes players not on the ice stand on the bench beside me, cheering wildly for the starting players. I think Beckett and the guys on the ice are doing well. I wouldn't know because I'm freezing, literally to death, and I hate nothing more or have less of a tolerance for than being cold. For all the schooling I've had, apparently, I didn't learn common sense. This is ice hockey. Of course it's going to be cold by the ice. Yet I'm wearing a silk blouse that has zero ability to hold in any body heat.

It's one of the rare October days that feels like summer in Michigan. They're my favorite—warm and breezy with the backdrop of the multihued autumn foliage. My slacks and blouse are appropriate attire for the weather outside this arena but not within.

Clamping my lips shut, I try to hide the chattering of my teeth and attempt to focus on the game and my players. Part of my job is noticing if someone favors a certain part of their body over the other, which could be a sign they're compensating because of a pulled muscle. The guys are tough and will play through anything. But I'm trying to show them if we catch tears and pulls early and start therapy, they're back to prime form sooner. Yet all they care about is staying on the ice.

At this moment, a player could be out there swinging his broken arm like a lasso, and I wouldn't notice. I can't focus on anything but how cold I am and, by extension, how disappointed I am in myself that I didn't think of this prior.

The equipment manager, Eddy, nudges my side with his elbow. "They're doing great! Aren't they?"

"Sure are!" I feign excitement.

"This is our year, Doc! You showed up at the right time." He pumps his arm in the air after one of the players did something... good, I'm guessing.

"Definitely. This is great!" I force the words out and cross my arms over my chest, clamping my lips shut as my teeth start to chatter again. I can't even jump up and down to get warm in my heels. It'd be a one-way ticket to spraining my own ankle.

The first period ends, and the guys head to the locker room to rest and refuel. I'm eager to follow when Coach Albright asks me to check on his nephew in the sound booth. Apparently, the kid thinks he cut off his finger. I grab my med bag and hurry up the stairs to the sound room.

The kid, here shadowing the sound guys for his high school "discovering careers" class, holds a bloody hand to his chest.

I snap the latex gloves onto my hands. "What happened?" Grabbing a towel, I wrap it around the injured hand. I need to clear off some of the blood to see what I'm dealing with.

"I was cutting my apple," the kid cries.

"Cutting an apple?" I question. His answer feels out of place in this environment.

One of the sound guys fills me in. "He brought his own snacks, including an apple and a knife. He sliced his finger when trying to cut his apple."

"How'd you get a knife through security?" It shouldn't be my first question, but I'm curious.

He shrugs. "I didn't go through security. I came in with my uncle."

"Right." I nod, dabbing at his hand with the towel. "Why an apple?"

"Because the food here is not healthy at all. I can't eat that stuff."

The coach's nephew is different from most high school boys I've worked with. "Makes sense. Well, good news is you did not cut your finger off, not even close. In fact, you don't need stitches."

"But all the blood." He stares at his hand, wide eyed.

"Fingers are one of the places on your body that bleed a lot. The amount of blood can be deceiving." I finish cleaning him up, put some antibiotic ointment on the cut, and wrap his finger in a Band-Aid. "You're good to go." I throw out the gauze and towel and discard my gloves in the trash.

"Wow. Okay. Thank you." The boy looks at his hand like he's grateful his finger is still there.

After a trip to the bathroom to wash my hands, it's almost time for the second period to start. It was so warm in the sound booth I forgot all about my torment. Yet as I descend the stairs and get closer to the ice, the air becomes more chilly, and I'm once again reminded of the torture that awaits.

Beckett is leaned over his skate, adjusting his laces. "Where were you?"

"Coach's nephew needed me."

"Oh." Beckett nods as if no more explanation is needed. He finishes up with his skate and reaches for something on the bench. "I brought you something." He hands me a navy blue Cranes jacket.

I could literally break down and cry. "Oh my gosh. You're my hero."

He leans over and gives me a kiss. "You know I'd do anything for you."

"Good luck out there."

"I don't need luck. I have talent." He winks and skates out onto the ice.

I shake my head with a chuckle. That man needs to learn how to be humble. Then again, if he were, he wouldn't be Beckett. I zip up the jacket and release a contented sigh. I'm immediately warm. The jacket is big on me and falls past my hips, bringing toasty relief to most of my body.

"Nice jacket." Eddy nods in approval. "Great number."

I look down at the white block number eighteen on my chest. I laugh and look up to find Beckett grinning like a fool out on the ice.

In the end, he got me to wear his number. I can't even be mad because I'm infinitely happier with this jacket on, and though I'm afraid to admit it, in more ways than one.

# CHAPTER
## TWENTY-THREE

ELENA

J aden and I are the last ones in the locker room. Hands outstretched behind him, he's propped up on the bench. His right leg is extended, resting atop a hard surface—and he has a heat compress on his knee.

He drops his head back, letting it fall between his shoulder blades. "You're killing me, Doc."

The team has been unanimously calling me Doc, and I'm so grateful to Beckett for making it clear that they were not allowed to address me as Hottie. No self-respecting sports med doctor should be referred to as such.

"No, I'm helping you. If you don't want your tendinitis to get worse, you have to take care of it." I grab the roll of athletic tape and a towel and walk over to Jaden.

He looks up at me. "I've been playing with it for years. It's nothing I can't handle."

"Yeah, well... you're lucky you're young. Your body bounces back more easily, but that won't always be the case. There's no reason you have to be in pain. We can manage it so it doesn't bother you."

"It barely hurts. I hardly notice it. But I am very aware that all the guys are out celebrating our win, and I'm stuck here. I don't think you realize how awesome the bars are here in Seattle." He pins me with a pleading stare.

I shake my head. "I'll have you out of here in two minutes."

"Good."

I remove the heating pad and towel the moisture off his knee. Ripping off a stretch of athletic tape, I apply it from his quad muscle to the skin below his knee to relieve some of the pull on that tendon. I repeat the taping on the other side of his knee. "We need to build up your quads. That big muscle is capable of doing the heavy lifting. When you strengthen them, they'll relieve a lot of the strain on these tendons and lessen your pain."

"Yeah, yeah. Got it. Sounds great, Doc. Now, am I good?"

Stepping back from the bench, I extend an arm toward the door. "Yes. You're free to go."

"Sweet." Hopping up, he grabs his jeans and quickly puts them on. "You going to join us at the bar?"

"Maybe."

He shoves his sock-clad feet into a pair of colorful Jordans. "You should. I'm not kidding. The bar life here is insane!"

Jaden hurries from the locker room. I lag behind, loading up my medical bag. Everything in me wants to go back to the hotel and crash. Flying back and forth for road games across the country and the three-hour time change is for the birds. If I were back in Michigan, I'd be in my bed asleep.

But the Cranes had an impressive victory, and Beckett made two of the goals. I should go celebrate with them, at least for a little while.

The energy of the guys is sure to wake me up. A month in, they're already having an impressive season, and the team morale has been high. They're all so sure that this is the year, and I really hope it is.

"This the one?" the Uber driver asks. I look out the window to the neon bar sign, and it matches the name Beckett sent me via text.

"Seems to be. Thank you." I step out of the car. The wind is brutally chilly on this Seattle night, and I hurry into the bar.

Pulling my phone out of my purse, I input a tip for the Uber driver and notice the email icon on the top of my screen. I vaguely remember receiving the email notification hours ago, but I was too busy to check it.

Music blares, and the Crane players and fans party throughout the space. The bar isn't what I'd imagined. Everything from the floor to the walls, chairs and tables are wood. The interior is a sea of brown with neon beer brand signs flashing along the walls. It's an odd design scheme, but I suppose the vibe is what counts.

I haven't been noticed yet, so I steal away to a far back corner to check my emails. There's a new email from my father's law firm. Interest piqued, I open it.

My eyes scan the words over and over. I read the text, but it takes a minute to register the message. Just to verify, I read the email one more time. The information hasn't changed.

Releasing a breath, I slide my phone into my purse.

*My father is dead.*

I'm not sure how I'm supposed to feel at this

moment, but I'm certain it's not this because I feel nothing. I wouldn't describe it as an indifference because even that seems too expressive. I'm emotionally void. There are no impending feelings of sadness or anything else. Before I flew out to Seattle, he was alive on this earth, and now he's not.

Grief is a strange thing, but the truth is I mourned my father or at least my dream of what I wanted him to be a long time ago. He and I have had a disconnect from the moment I was born. I feel as if I should be sad, but I'm not. I should hold regrets that we'll never mend our fences, but I don't. Accepting the reality of our relationship was a crucial step to healing, and it's been many years since I've come to terms with what my father was and what he could never be.

Still… he was my last living parent, and I should feel something.

It's not until Beckett crosses my mind that I feel something. Only this time, the barrage of emotions are so strong that I'm in a state of complete overwhelm.

"I see you found the best seat in the place." I look up to see the PR and social media director, Penelope Stellars. "I was hiding back here a bit ago but had to go take care of something. Do you mind if I join you?"

My cordial autopilot clicks on, and I smile. "Sure."

I'm a professional at slipping into a polite state of fakeness because I've done it for years. As a single mother with limited funds, there have been so many times I had to act the part even when my world felt like it was crashing down around me. It's weird being back here. I haven't visited this state of delusion since I had to talk to Beckett about his knee in the hospital room right after my daughter's electricity had been turned off.

"How are the guys?" I ask.

She rolls her eyes. "Awful. I hate road games. At home, I have a good relationship with the reporters and bar staff. Others help keep everyone in check. But on the road? Every night is another mess." She sighs.

"What would happen if one of the guys did something stupid and ended up on social media?"

She clasps her hands together and sets them on the wooden table between us. "I mean, technically, nothing. They're all grown men with the ability to act appropriately. If one of them gets wasted and gets in a bar fight, it's not the end of the world. I wouldn't lose my job or anything like that. Yet I take my position very seriously. When I agree to do something, I make sure it's done right. The Cranes jersey sales are higher than ever. Our home games are sold out. And you saw it tonight. Even on road games three hours away, there was a sea of navy and white jerseys. It pays to keep a good reputation."

"The organization is lucky to have you."

She huffs out a laugh. Her long, manicured nails tap on the table. "Tell me about it."

"I bet Beckett makes a lot of messes for you to clean up."

She looks over her shoulder, and I follow her gaze to where Beckett stands with a beer in his hand. A group of women circle him, and whatever they're saying must be hilarious because he's laughed at least a dozen times since I got here.

Returning her attention to me, she shakes her head. "Actually, no. Beckett's a great guy. He likes to party, but he's respectful and keeps it together for the most part. He's like a golden retriever. He's cute, funny, and extremely friendly. He messes up sometimes, but it's all little things, like a golden who chews on a shoe when he's not supposed to. It's never anything I can't handle. Just like a golden retriever isn't out there mauling off the leg of a little old lady, he's not causing any serious damage."

My eyes widen. "Well, that's good. Are there guys that would cause damage? They all seem sweet."

Her lips press into a line, and she inhales through her nose. She quirks a brow. "Have you met Gunner Dreven?"

"Yeah, he's quiet and grumpy, but he seems pretty harmless."

"He has a temper, and when you're as big as he is with a short fuse, it's never good."

"Yikes. Well, okay, I didn't realize that."

She raises her shoulders. "I've kept him out of trouble, but the potential is there. I swear, he alone is a full-time job."

"Do you mind if I share an opinion?" Her eyes narrow.

"Um… sure." I shrug.

"I never pictured someone like you and someone like Beckett together. I'm happy for you, of course. I don't mean it negatively at all. It's just an odd pairing."

I chuckle. "Well, you're not wrong. We are an odd pairing."

I keep it at that. While sometimes a little too serious, the woman sitting across from me has been very nice. She's welcomed me into the organization and has been very helpful. But I'm not ready to open up about the complexities of the relationship between my faux husband and me.

And now that my father is no longer with us, my soon-to-be ex-faux husband.

"If you'll excuse me, I'm going to say hi to the guys." I slide out from the hard booth seat.

As I approach Beckett, it starts to really sink in.

My father is gone. All of this can be over.

Halting my approach, I take in the scene. All these

twentysomethings—drinking, laughing, and celebrating their victory—fill the bar. I have no desire to be
among them. Not that I'm not proud of the guys or
enjoy their company, but I'm tired. I want to be in my
jammies, at home, bingeing the *Gilmore Girls* for the
hundredth time. I don't want to be doing shots from
someone's belly button.

Bash smiles, shot glass in his mouth. The woman
lying across the bar pulls her Cranes jersey back down,
sits up, and raises her hands in the air. Those who
surround her cheer along. Taking the shot glass from
his mouth, he tips it toward the girl and gives her a
wink.

Anxiety fills my chest. If I'm here too much longer,
I'll witness Beckett taking shots from women's belly
buttons, and that's not something I want to see.

I don't belong here. Put me in a locker room with
my med bag and some sprained muscles or in a sound
box with a crying teen who thinks he chopped his
finger off. Those I can handle without a second
thought. Navigating the team celebrating in a bar with
liquor and puck bunnies—I cannot.

Beckett still hasn't seen me, and I'm relieved. I'm
overwhelmed with the thoughts running through my
head and need time to process them. Staring at that
beautiful man is something I will never grow tired of.
There's no question that Beckett is gorgeous. He simply

is. Beyond that, though, he's kind, caring, and so very loving. I'd be remiss if I didn't admit that he's also sexy as hell. The way in which our bodies come together is so incredible, books should be written about it. But marriage is a lifetime commitment, and its entire foundation can't just be good sex.

Beckett did me a favor and gave up so much to marry me and ensure I received my inheritance. Just because he's a good guy doesn't mean I should hold him to our Vegas vows for the rest of his life. And I don't know... maybe he doesn't want me to.

He seems happy, and I can't deny I've been happier than I ever remember being. However, just because we turned an awkward situation into something great doesn't mean we're bound to it forever. We haven't spoken about the end of this arrangement. It was easier to live in and enjoy the moments as they passed. Now, we have to address it. He promised me a fake marriage. He didn't promise me forever, and even if he had, I can't say I'd take it. We're two different people in vastly different stages of our lives.

There's no doubt I'll miss him terribly. I've grown comfortable with him in my life. But we both knew this had an expiration date, and I don't see a reason to prolong the inevitable.

A female fan wraps her arms around Beckett's

middle and leans into him as her friend holds up a cell phone and takes a picture.

*Yeah, I don't belong here.*

I shouldn't mourn for someone I never had, for something that was never meant to be. I sneak out of the bar as quietly as I came in.

It was always going to end.

I just wish it didn't hurt so much.

# CHAPTER
## TWENTY-FOUR

BECKETT

C ade nudges my shoulder. "I'm sure it's fine, man. I wouldn't worry."

My knee continues to bounce, and I ignore him. It's better than telling him everything that I will if I open my mouth. A plane full of my teammates and the Cranes staff isn't the place to announce my fake marriage.

But he's wrong.

It's so far from fine.

When Jaden showed up at the bar complaining about the fuss that Elena had made over his knee, I knew she'd be along any minute. When an hour had passed and she hadn't shown, I texted her to check in. I wasn't all that worried at that point. I figured she had gone back to the room to crash. She had admitted to being exhausted earlier. When another hour and several more unanswered texts went by, I left the bar to head back to our room, fully expecting to find her sound asleep in the bed.

But that's not what I found.

I found a note stating she took a commercial flight home to take care of some things.

These "things" she has to take care of are bad news. Of course they are. If it were something positive, she would've answered my texts instead of leaving a handwritten note for me to find hours later. When it was too late to do or say anything to talk her out of whatever she's up to.

Though I don't want to admit it, I already know.

*I already fucking know.*

Her father's gone, and she's leaving me. I feel it down in my soul. I'm not a panicky person, and I don't freak out about much, but I'm suffocating on this plane. I can't get back fast enough.

This was all meant to be temporary. But who were we kidding? Elena and I are as permanent as they come. I love her more than I knew was possible to love another person. Not one cell in my body wants this to end. This hasn't been fake, at least for me, for quite some time. In fact, the moment I said I do with Elvis as our witness, I was all in.

"Beck." Cade puts his hand on my knees to halt the incessant tapping. "What's wrong? You're starting to worry me. Is there something I should know? Something you're not telling me?"

Emotion wells in my eyes, and I feel as if I'm truly about to lose my shit. "Not here."

He removes his hand. "Okay. Do you need anything? Water?"

"No. I just need to get home."

"Another hour and we'll be landing. It'll be okay," he says again. While annoying, I can't hold it against him. If he knew the truth, he would know that if Elena leaves me—I'll be the furthest from okay.

The minutes tick by as slow as humanly possible until finally, the plane lands. Without a word to anyone, I race to my car and drive toward our condo. It's almost noon. I hate that I missed the last commercial flight back to Michigan. Coach has a rule that the team flies back from road games on our chartered plane together. He hasn't made many exceptions to that rule over the years. Had there been the opportunity to take another flight home, I would have— Coach's rules be damned. As it is, this was the best I could do, and it gave Elena the whole night without me to do what she came back for.

I don't remember the drive home, parking, or running up the sidewalk to my condo. But I know as soon as I turn the key and open the door that she's gone.

Most of her things are in storage, but the little pieces of her that existed here have created a void, making the space feel empty. Her phone charger with the long purple cord that she left plugged in by the sofa is missing. Her favorite mug, with a photo collage of Ariana when she was a toddler, that Elena hung on a hook by the coffee pot is gone. The soft fleece throw I bought for her to keep on the couch because she's always cold, the blanket she uses every day, is still folded in its place on the back of the sofa, and my rage builds. She only took the items she came with and left what I gave her as if that moment in time had never happened. In less than twelve hours, she's erased me from her life.

I already know what I'll find in the bedrooms, so it's not a shock when I discover them empty of her clothes and toiletries. She packed up what little she had here and left me before I could beg her to stay.

I sit on my bed. Shoulders slumping, I drop my elbows to my knees, and my hands hold my face. I breathe deeply, in and out, trying to wrap my mind around it all. Things were so good between us that I was naive enough to think I'd never be in this place.

We never openly discussed continuing our relationship, but I'd just assumed we would. Why would she want to end what we have? She's been here. She knows how great we are together. It doesn't make sense.

Even now, after she left me in Seattle to rush home and move out of our home, I don't believe it's real. A world in which Elena and I aren't together doesn't feel real. Dueling emotions rage inside, and I struggle with what to feel. Do I break down, cry, and lose my shit? Or hold it together and go find her? I suppose it's pretty obvious when I lay it out like that.

I stand from my bed and twist my torso, cracking my back. I barely slept last night and could use some shut-eye, but I have to talk to Elena. A note card, folded in half with my name on the front, sits atop the nightstand. I open it.

*Beckett,*

*We both knew this would end.*
   *Thank you for five beautiful months together.*
   *You're a good guy, and I'm grateful to call you a friend.*

*See you at work.*

. . .

*Doc*

"What in the actual fuck?" I yell, crumpling the note and tossing it across the room.

There's so much about this goodbye letter that has me consumed with fury that I can hardly see straight. *Doc?* Who is she kidding with that? I'm not one of the guys. I haven't referred to her as Doc since we decided to get married in the first place. *Friend?* I am so much more than that title allows for, and she knows it. She fucking knows it.

There's a loud knock on my door, and I can tell by the fist hitting the wood that it's Cade.

I open the door to find Cade and Iris.

"You have to tell us what's going on. We're worried sick about you!" Iris rushes in and throws her arms around me. In a feeble attempt, I give her a half hug, patting her back with one hand.

"Why not? Take a seat." My words lack emotion, and my mouth is stuck in a frown.

"Listen. I'm really fucking tired and even more angry. So let me just get this all out before you ask questions. Okay? Do you agree to that?" I pin Iris with a stare because we all know she's the one I'm referring to.

She clamps her lips shut and does the whole invisible key and lock thing.

For the first time since I concocted this plan, I talk to someone other than Elena about it. Pacing back and forth in front of the sofa where they sit, I tell my best friend and sister everything. I start at the very beginning and end with the dumbass note I just read. I explain how it started as a simple attraction and wanting to help a person out who needed someone to our wedding and subsequently falling in love with her. I give them all the details, and it's freeing. I haven't been able to keep a secret from these two since we were kids. They've been my support system and my sounding board my entire life. I gave up that part of myself when I agreed to keep this secret for Elena, and now that I'm finally coming clean, a weight lifts off my chest.

I stop walking and turn to face them. They both stare, wearing expressions somewhere between shock and pity. I wave my hand, giving permission to speak. "Go ahead."

Iris stands from the sofa. She presses her fingers to her temples as if her brain can hardly contain the information. "I knew it. I knew something was off. You haven't been yourself. You would never have flown off to Vegas to get married, especially without inviting us.

None of it added up. I mean, I didn't guess you were marrying her so she could inherit her father's money, but I just knew something wasn't right!" she says.

I dip my head back and sigh. "Yes, we've established that you *knew it,* but what do I do now? Cade?"

Cade shakes his head. "I'm sorry, man. I'm still processing. That was a lot of information to receive in two minutes."

"The whole thing was crazy. As I listen to myself give you the details, I realize how insane it must all sound, and I guess it was. But that doesn't change the fact that I truly fell in love with her. Our start wasn't ideal or in any way normal, but I love her. I really do." I jerk my fingers through my hair.

"Hey." Iris steps toward me and takes my hands in hers. "Do you want to stay married to her?"

"Yeah," I choke out. "I can't imagine spending the rest of my life with anyone else."

She shrugs and gives me a smile. "Well, then you know what you have to do."

"Get her back."

"Absolutely." She smiles. "This is like something straight out of a romance novel, Beck."

"Yeah!" I pull my sister into a hug. I've wasted hours ridden with anxiety, fear, and anger when the solution is as simple as they come. "I'm going to get my wife back."

Maybe our love story is like one that my sister likes to read in her romance novels, but at the same time, it's completely different. The amount of love that I feel for Elena, no matter how well written, could never be contained to an entire novel. It's too great.

# CHAPTER
## TWENTY-FIVE

BECKETT

I feel like death as I step into the locker room to get ready for practice. Sleep has evaded me since our night in Seattle, and I'm a walking zombie at this point. I spent the entire day yesterday looking for Elena. After my chat with Iris and Cade, I was pumped to find my wife and convince her that our marriage was worth saving.

But my wife had other plans.

She ignored every call, text, and email. She blocked me from seeing her location on all social media apps, and she didn't use her credit card or name wherever she stayed. She covered all her bases and made sure I couldn't find her.

Today, physically exhausted and emotionally spent, I don't know how to feel about it all. Why did she work so hard to make sure I couldn't locate her? Did she really value our time together so little that she honestly thought a couple of lines scribbled on a folded note card was an adequate goodbye?

I dropped everything and lied to everyone I love for her. I have gone above and beyond not only to make sure her secret was safe but to make sure she was happy. I deserve more than this. She's silencing me when I'm owed a rebuttal. Marriage... and divorce is a two-way street. As much as she wants things ended her way, that's not reality. I get a say, and while she may not agree and it might not change the outcome, I have a voice nonetheless.

Cade shuts his locker. "You okay, man?"

"Not even close." I hit my locker, and it slams shut.

He slaps me on the back. "Let's go work it off."

"Yeah."

As long as I can remember, there's been nothing that hockey can't fix. For me, it's the ultimate endorphin-releasing activity. But I can't say it's going to help today.

Elena enters the locker room. She flicks her eyes to me for a second before she hurries into her office and closes the door.

I shake my head with a scoff. If she thinks a door

will keep me away, she's wrong. Luckily for her, I don't have time for a conversation of this magnitude right now. I have work to do. She's taken a lot from me, but she won't take away my first love. As tired as I am and as shitty as I feel, I'll give my all on the ice as I always do. The urge to crumple, scream, fall apart, and cry over my lost love is there. The need is so heavy it's suffocating. Yet somewhere deep within my soul is the strength to fight those feelings off.

Hockey is the love of my life. From the moment I got my first stick and plastic net for Christmas at the age of five, there's been no turning back. I won't lose it, especially for something that, according to her, was never real in the first place.

If there were an award for compartmentalizing, I would be the freaking champion—gold metal material. Elena has made herself scarce this entire week, and I've been too busy to track her down. We had a four-game week, which are always brutal. One of the games included Pittsburgh, which, up until playoffs last season, I would've never considered our rival or competition—but that obviously changed.

Though I shouldn't, I hold guilt where that loss to

Pittsburgh is concerned. Had I avoided the dick and not let him hit me into the boards and fuck up my knee, Cade and Bash wouldn't have lost it and ended up in the penalty box, and we wouldn't have been down players during the final minutes of the game, allowing Pittsburgh to score and break our tie to win the round and effectively end our chances at the Cup.

I love Elena, and I still believe that I can make this right when I get the chance to talk to her. But this mess can't come at a cost to the team. Piling on more guilt over losses isn't something I'm willing to do.

Elena has kept busy during our home games and sent our PTs as her replacements for our road games. It's not unusual, as our old doctor, Hootie, rarely came along on road games. It is, however, atypical for Elena. Up until this week, she's been at every Cranes practice and game.

We've played extremely well this week, which has made focusing on my career and not on my love life easier. We lost our first game against Toronto, but won the next two against Boston and Pittsburgh. If we can pull out a win tonight against Chicago, it will have been a successful week. When we're back in Michigan tomorrow, I'll confront Elena in the penthouse suite of the hotel in Ann Arbor, where she's been hiding out all week. This information was just given to me by the PI I had tail her.

Nothing says true love like hiring a private investigator to follow your wife so you can have a conversation with her.

I finish lacing up my skates.

"Ready to do this?" Bash asks.

"Oh, I'm ready, Cookie."

He sighs. "You gotta add the monster, or it sounds dumb and makes me look like an idiot."

I laugh. "I don't know if that really helps."

"Suck it up, Cookie. Let's go," TJ Maxx claps Bash on his pads and steps onto the ice.

"Monster. Cookie Monster," Bash calls after him, following him onto the ice.

I look at Cade. He chuckles under his breath, amused. "Let's go have some fun." He holds his gloved hand out to me, and I bump his fist with mine.

"Absolutely."

The arena is packed. It's a road game in Chicago, but almost half the crowd sports Cranes colors, and that makes it all that more exciting. Chicago is a formidable opponent, but we're relentless. Max and Jaden are on the top of their defense game, and Dreven is the beast of a goalie he always is. Cade, Bash, and I hit the puck to one another in effortless precision, scoring an impressive five goals by the time the final buzzer sounds, ending the game in a five-to-three win.

This season is ours. When I imagine the playoffs,

our win plays so vividly in my mind it feels tangible. The Cup is ours. This is the right team at the right time. When we're on the ice, it's magic. All I have to do is get my wife back tomorrow, and this will undoubtedly be the best year of my life.

# CHAPTER
## TWENTY-SIX

ELENA

For years, I've wondered what it would feel like to make it, to reach the destination I've been striving for. I've dreamed about it, archived pictures in the vision board in my mind, and looked forward to the day when I would be happy. The day all my dreams would come true.

This is not to say I would've traded my life with Ariana for anything. We struggled, but we were happy. She was enough, but as I worked for more, I couldn't help but dream about what it would be like when I was living a life that was more than enough.

The thing is, I'm here. This is it, I think. This is my more than enough, yet I've never been so miserable. I'm constantly questioning my choices. My mind knows I'm doing the right thing, but why does it feel so awful if this is what is meant to be? And when will this torture end?

According to the plastic stick in my hand with the blue plus sign, not anytime soon.

Leaning my back against the bathroom wall, I slide down until I sit against the tiled floor. Knees bent, I hug my legs to my chest as the tears fall in streams. I'm consumed with pain and regret. How did I get here?

I have more money than any single person should possess. I'm working at my dream job. My daughter is happy and thriving. Yet here I sit, wallowing in self-pity and getting ready to start the single-mom journey all over again at the age of forty. Where was my common sense? Why didn't I get on birth control?

Beckett and I used a condom almost every time, save for a few heat-of-the-moment encounters in the shower. Even then, he pulled out. We were careful. At forty years old, I didn't want to start birth control and mess with my hormones when I wouldn't need it for long. I know neither method we used was a hundred percent, but I figured along with my age, it was sufficient.

I'm so alone and drowning in sadness, and the one person I want to talk to, I can't. Beckett, being the fixer he is, would accept responsibility for me and the baby —no questions asked. Yet the entire reason I left was to give him the happiness and life he deserved. He doesn't want this. I want someone who is at the same place in life as me, who is ready to settle down, who doesn't want to party late into the night, and isn't the whore of the team. I'm not going to guilt Beckett into a life he doesn't want, only for him to wake up one day, a few years down the road, and resent me for stealing his youth.

Beckett and I are compatible, and we do share a deep love for one another. I know this to be true. There are just too many factors at play that make our pairing less than ideal.

I love him. I truly do. And that's why I won't trap him.

Had we met under different circumstances and in another life, our love story would be epic. In this life, we simply can't work.

Avoiding him all week has been exhausting. When I started feeling sick after Seattle, I'd assumed it was the stress of the breakup. It takes a lot out of a person to avoid the one person they crave. I needed some time and distance between us. Beckett required a few days of separation so that when I did talk to him, he'd listen to reason. I can't put it off anymore. It's too draining. But now this new development will require a lot more finesse when I go to explain.

Perhaps I'll deal with the breakup first, and in a few

months' time, when Beckett has healed and moved on with his life, I'll let him know about the baby. I don't expect anything from him. He didn't choose this. He's here because of me. He's here because of the millions sitting in a bank account with my name on it. Now, it hardly seems worth it. Some things—in fact, most things—are so much more valuable than money.

Tossing the pregnancy test into the garbage can, I will myself off the bathroom floor. As far as restroom floors go, it's pretty nice, but it's not the most comfortable place to have a nervous breakdown. I snatch the box of tissue from the fancy faux-rusted metal box that sits atop the granite countertop and take it with me. I look around my hotel room and sigh. All this luxury and not a single service looks appealing. I yearn for Beckett's couch and the fuzzy blanket he bought for me.

I pass the bowl of fresh fruit, one of the perks of this fancy suite. They're probably charging me fifty bucks an apple and working the price into the extravagant daily rate of this place. Not that it matters to me. I never have to worry about money again. Sure, motel rooms frequented by cockroaches may no longer be in my future, but apparently, happiness isn't either—so all in all, an even trade.

I fall back onto the floral upholstered sofa with a groan. I'm sure this thing is designer and cost way more than it should have, but it's not remotely comfortable. I blink away the steady river of tears that falls from my eyes, dabbing my face with tissues. There's no sense in attempting to stop the waterworks at this point. There's so much misery festering under my skin that it demands to be released.

I'm so alone. I miss him. I need him. Somehow, this time around seems more miserable than the first. It doesn't make sense because when I left home after becoming pregnant with Ari, I was in dire straits and struggling to put a roof over my head on a daily basis. The same stressors are no longer part of my life, but the ache in my heart feels greater. I truly never thought I'd have the chance to be a mom again. I definitely never dreamed that if I was fortunate enough to get another chance that I'd be doing it alone.

A knock sounds at my door. Stupid room service people. They're always stopping by with fruit baskets, fresh flowers, or baked goods. I don't want any of it. "No, thank you! I'm good!" I call out.

There's more knocking.

I hate this place and its intrusive deliveries and uncomfortable sofas. With a grumble, I force myself up from the sofa. Let the room service guy see me in all my puffy-eyed, tear-soaked, snotty glory. Maybe he'll realize then when I say I don't want any of the perks of this suite, I mean it.

I swing the door open, and the room service guy is nowhere to be found.

It's Beckett.

His chest heaves, and brows furrow with anger. He takes me in, and his features soften. Stepping into the hotel room, he closes the door behind him. It's so good to see him. My lip trembles, and the tears stream down my cheeks.

"Elena..." My name is a plea and an accusation all rolled into one. He wraps his strong arms around me and pulls me into his chest. He holds me tight and kisses my head while I cry all over his shirt. "I'm. So. Mad. At. You." His words are a staccato, uttered between kisses.

In true Beckett form, he pushes his needs, his questions aside and comforts me. He sees me hurting, and he wants to fix it, and as the weak person I am, I let him.

He leads me to the sofa and pulls me onto his lap. I circle my arms around his neck and bury my face. I can't look at him. My embarrassment idles, burning the surface of my skin. But I can't resist his love. I need it.

Time passes in a blur, and he holds me as I cry. Though it seemed impossible, my tears eventually run dry. There's no avoiding him now. Panic rises as I think about what I should do and say. I climb off his lap and scoot back until I'm on the opposite side of the sofa.

Grabbing a handful of tissues, I clean up my face and blow my nose.

"I'm sorry." Regret scalds my words, and more emotions sting the back of my eyes. I drag the tissue across my eyes and take several deep, fortifying breaths. "How did you find me?"

"I had you followed." He works hard to keep his face void of emotion, but I see it anyway, and the sadness behind his eyes breaks my heart.

"You had me followed?" The vitriol I want to feel for such an intrusion doesn't come.

He twists and leans against the arm of the sofa, facing me. His palms turn up. "What other choice did I have, Elena? You've been skillfully avoiding me for a week. You break up with me via a note card after skipping out on me in Seattle. I'm owed a conversation, at least."

My chin dips. "I know."

"So why? Why are you doing this? Why are you hiding from me?"

I circle my head around, my stiff neck cracks, and I breathe in through my nose. "Well, the easier question to answer is because I wanted to give us both time to process the inevitable. I thought with some time and distance, the breakup would be easier to accept."

He furrows his brows. "Why are we breaking up? We were happy."

"Yeah, and maybe we would've been happy together for a little while, but in the long run, you and I won't work. I've told you that from the beginning. We're too different. We're at completely separate places in our lives. You know, I wanted to talk to you in Seattle, but I saw you at the bar with your teammates and fans, and it made it even more clear that we're not in the same space. I'm a lot older than you and as a result in a different stage in my life. Before I came, you were the life of the party, the team whore."

"Elena," he groans, annoyed.

"Look. I'm not saying that is a bad thing. I'm saying that you changed so much to be with me for a few months for this fake marriage. I hated it then, but I'm certainly not going to make you change everything about yourself in the long term. Real love, the kind that lasts, is between two people who meet one another exactly where they are. We're not in the same place." He starts to argue, but I hold up a hand to stop him. "I know that the love we share is real. We obviously have a great connection, but those two things will only get us so far. I have no doubt that you'll offer to change everything about yourself to be with me, but I don't want that for you. Because being someone you're not isn't sustainable. Eventually, we'd crumble, and you'd resent me for stealing years of your life from you."

"No." His facial features harden. "You do not get to

tell me *who I am.* Because clearly, after all our time together, you don't have a clue. I know who I am, and that is someone who is irrevocably in love with you. The partying and sleeping around? Those were things I did but not who I am. I don't need to stay out late at parties or sleep with countless women to be happy. I need you. Full stop."

"You say that now—"

He cuts me off. "Because it's true, and it will be true forever. Look, I get that you think you're so wise because you're older than me, but in reality, it's the complete opposite. You are so afraid of losing control. You've made it your mission since you left home to be in sole control of your life. The intensity of the love we share scares you to death. That's the thing about true love, Elena. It is scary as hell. It consumes you and leaves you vulnerable. A hell of a lot of faith is required when you're in love with someone, and you have to trust in that person to be there for you, to protect you, to safeguard your heart because being all in is a risk. It will always be a gamble. There is no way to guarantee your partner won't shatter your heart. Life happens. People change. People die. Love is never a hundred percent risk-free. That's just not the way life works."

He scoots across the sofa, closing the gap between us. He takes my hands in his. "I love you, Elena. I don't know exactly when it happened. Part of me feels I loved you the moment I met you. I don't care that you're thirteen years older than me. My love for you is soul-deep. We have a connection, and it's unlike anything I've ever felt. I know you feel it, too. Love doesn't have guidelines. It doesn't care about age, race, occupation, or any other descriptor—it's all about the connection. I'm certain that I can search for the rest of my life and I'll never find someone who makes me feel the way that you do. If you don't feel the same way, then I'll be forced to accept it, but I know you do. I love you so much. Just let us be happy. It doesn't have to be this hard."

I shake my head. "I don't want to go to bars after a game."

A smile tugs at his lips. "Then don't. I can stay back with you or just go and hang out with the guys without you for a little bit and then come home. That's something we can discuss. The cool thing about marriage is the couple has the ability to talk things out and decide what's in the best interest of everyone involved. It's called compromise."

"The team hasn't stopped talking about your bye week vacation this year. What if I don't want to go drink for a week straight in some exotic location. You'll stay back with me, and there will be regrets."

"Yeah, maybe some of the guys will miss me and wish I was there, but me personally, I won't have a single regret. Here's the thing. I did all those things—partying, sleeping around, planning extravagant bye week vacations—because that's what I had. Now, I have you, and I'm being completely honest when I say I'd choose you over all of that a hundred times over. What don't you understand about this? I love you. I choose you. I want you. All that"—he waves his hand in a circle between us—"was fun. But you"—he presses his palm to my chest—"are everything. Every. Fucking. Thing. Elena."

Tears cascade down my face once more. "This is why we needed time apart. It's hard to argue with you when you say beautiful things."

"You mean, it's hard to argue against the truth, and not the one you've concocted in your mind but the actual truth that you and I, despite all our differences, are meant for one another? And maybe we always were? That your path led you to that professor who was friends with Hootie and got you the job that led you to my hospital room that led us to get to know each other while I healed and be together when you got that letter that crushed you, which gave me the idea to get married in the first place, and through this fake marriage fall madly in love with one another? Call it kismet, destiny, fate, luck, or fortune, but the fact remains—we're meant to be together."

He drops his hand from my chest and takes my

hand in his. He pulls it toward him and places my hand against his chest. I feel his rapidly beating heart against my palm. "I have one fucking heart, and it was destined to love you. Only you."

I swallow the lump of emotion in my throat and nod.

"Question is." He brings my hand up to his lips and kisses it. "Elena, will you please not divorce me?"

I laugh through my tears and shake my head. "I won't divorce you."

"I love you," he says.

"I love you, too." I jump toward him, throwing my arms around his neck. He falls back onto the sofa, and my face hovers over his. Not able to wait another second, I crash my lips to his.

# CHAPTER
## TWENTY-SEVEN

BECKETT

All is right in the world again. Every bit of fear or anger I held over a future without Elena has vanished with a single kiss. I knew she was stuck in her head and creating a narrative that wasn't accurate. Everything I said to her is true. I don't care about any of the stuff she's worried about. My attention is singularly focused, and it's a hundred percent locked in on her.

We kiss until my lips ache, and after a few minutes, she pulls away. "I missed you so much." Her face hovers a breath away from mine.

"Me too. Please don't ever leave me again."

She sighs and gives me a sad smile before pushing off me.

We sit up on the sofa.

I look around. "Nice place you have here."

"Yeah, well, I am a millionaire now." She scrunches her lips and raises her shoulders.

I scoot next to her and wrap my arm around her shoulders. Leaning in, I kiss the top of her head. "Yeah. How did everything go down with your father?"

"Well, I got the email that he had passed when I got to the bar in Seattle. I came home, packed up, and met with my father's lawyers that morning."

My body bristles when she mentions packing up, but I don't say anything. I'm eager to put it behind us.

She continues, "It was pretty easy. All the accounts were transferred over to me, along with the estate, and all his businesses."

"What are you going to do with the businesses? He must have dozens of factories around the world?"

"Well, I hired a business manager who will be in charge of ensuring they all run smoothly. The current staff and managers will stay on the payroll. I hope business will continue as usual and my father's death won't make a difference in their lives. I thought briefly about shutting everything down or selling, but I couldn't do that. Cortez Industries employs tens of thousands of people who rely on these jobs. I want to make sure they have job security, and the only way to do that is to keep it running business as usual. I'm definitely not against selling someday, but it has to be to someone I trust. I spoke to Diane."

"Diane?" I question.

"Yeah, I had a few of my earlier classes with her at the University of Michigan, the pre-req stuff, before I broke off into the medical requirements. We've kept in touch over the years through email. She has a law and business degree and is a great person. She's contracted out to help failing businesses. She's great at what she does. Cortez Industries isn't failing, but I hired her to be the business manager because I trust her, and I know she'll do right by me and the employees. Per my request, she's already looking into how to do companywide raises and healthcare coverage improvements. My father's profit margins were ridiculously high, so there is no reason why more money isn't going to the people who keep these factories running. Diane is also looking into getting rid of some of the useless managers and CFOs who were friends of my father's but don't add any value to the company. She sent out a way for employees to anonymously voice their complaints, and it's crazy how badly some people were being treated and how poorly some of these higher-ups are performing."

"Wow, you've been busy this week. I thought you were just avoiding me."

She smiles. "No… I mean, yes, I was avoiding you, but I did have legitimate stuff to take care of."

"Are you going to have a service for your father?"

"No. He's been cremated and is buried beneath the monstrous eyesore of a headstone he had commissioned per his wishes. He didn't have any friends, only associates. Now that he's gone, and they can't gain anything from his favor, I'm sure they couldn't care less about attending a service."

"Well, I'm glad it's over, and despite everything, I'm glad it brought us together." I squeeze her shoulder.

She snuggles into my side and lays her face against my chest. "Yeah, I still don't know why he made that clause about me getting married. I thought after he passed, I'd receive a letter of explanation or something, a reason as to why he's done what he's done, but there was nothing. He left no apologies or letters of any kind. He's just gone, and I still don't know why he was the way he was. It's unsettling."

I kiss the top of her head. "That's how it is with some people. They're just evil for the sake of being so, and there's no rhyme or reason."

"I guess it was just his final attempt at control. He lived and breathed power. He was always in charge, and I'm assuming found some sort of validation at being the most formidable person in the room. I was the one person he wasn't able to bend to his will, and maybe he wanted to know he could do it one last time. It's kind of disgusting, right? He's dying, and he wants to prove he can still control me? He doesn't want to get to know me or my daughter; he wants what he's always wanted, and that's to control my life. I've thought it through a lot, and it's the only thing that makes sense."

"Well, he's gone. You don't have to worry about him anymore. We're together and staying together..." I quirk a brow.

"Yes, we're staying together." Elena grins.

"Okay then. Life is good."

"I have something else to tell you," she says.

I smile. "I have something to tell you, too."

She pulls her legs up and sits cross-legged, facing me. "You go first."

I question her, and she insists, so I start in on the project I've been working on for a while now. "About a month ago, I met with your dad's private investigator."

"What? How? Why?" she rattles off one-word questions.

"First, I met with your dad. The meeting was very short. I needed some information, and I figured your father would've only hired the best. I mean, the P.I. had to be good if you were afraid that even what we said over our cell phones wasn't safe. Your father gave me

Bill's name and private number. I was planning on paying Bill myself, but your father said he had Bill on retainer and still had quite the credit with Bill, like several hundred thousands' worth. He told me to use that up first since he wouldn't be needing his services anymore."

Elena's brows furrow. "That doesn't seem like my father."

I shrug. "It sounds weird, but when I told him why I wanted Bill, he seemed almost pleased."

"Are you sure you met with my father? The man you're describing, giving and happy, doesn't add up."

I huff out a laugh. "I'm not saying he was happy by any stretch of the word, but I just got the sense that he was pleased."

She leans in. "So why did you need a P.I.?"

I breathe in and nerves build in my chest. "Okay. I'm not going to go into detail because, to be honest, the details are quite horrible and make me incredibly ill. But I had him look into your cousin."

"What?" she gasps.

I raise my hands, palms out. "Hear me out. Ever since that day in your office when I saw you crumple and the brief overview you gave of the horrors experienced at the hands of your cousin, I couldn't get it out of my head. I couldn't imagine anyone hurting a young, sweet Elena. It made my blood boil. And I've realized anyone who could hurt you that way is inherently evil, and people like that are always that way. There's no redemption for that behavior. I knew that chances were he'd hurt others. So I had Bill gather information, follow him, take surveillance footage—all of it, until we could get enough evidence for a search warrant. And we did. One of my father's lawyer buddies from school and the top prosecuting lawyer in Michigan for these cases took the case. The warrant gave law enforcement access to his home and computers, and as I figured there would be, there was a mountain of evidence on his computer. Your cousin is sitting in a jail cell as we speak, and with the case we have on him, he will be in prison for the rest of his life."

Tears fill Elena's eyes, and her voice trembles. "You really did that?"

"Of course I did. He hurt someone I love, and I protect those I love. You will never have to worry about seeing him or accidentally running into him for the rest of your life. He will die in prison, which is better than he deserves."

She cups my face in her hands. "I don't know what I did to deserve someone like you, Beckett, but you are the sweetest, funniest, most loving, and loyal man I've ever met. You deserve everything you've ever wanted. I want you to have the world."

"You are my world."

Tears fall down her face. "I can never thank you enough."

I kiss her forehead. "You don't have to thank me. I did it because I love you, and you deserve some peace. As my wife, you need to know that I would do anything for you. I'd give up anything. I'd go anywhere."

"I just hope I truly make you as happy as you make me."

"I promise, you do. Please believe me."

# CHAPTER TWENTY-EIGHT

## ELENA

I look into Beckett's eyes, and I see nothing but the raw truth. Despite our differences, he loves me. He chooses us and the life we'll have together. Doubts still simmer under the surface, little voices that urge me to question all the ways in which we're different, but I can't ignore the love we share because he's right. If I do —I doubt I'll ever find it again. This deep love doesn't come around often, and I can't lose it.

He's a grown man, and if he says he'll never regret us, I have to believe it. More so, I want to trust in his words because I could barely stomach a week without him. I can't imagine a lifetime.

One of the greatest things about Beckett is his ability to love. His love is fierce and relentless. Once you've lived in his light, it'd be miserable to exist in the darkness without him.

But there's still another matter to discuss, and while I think his response will be favorable, I can't be certain. I'm expecting a lot of change, and fast.

"What is it?" Beckett holds my hands in his. "There's something else. You still aren't convinced, are you?" The panic in his expression grows.

I shake my head. "It's not that." My chin dips to my chest, and I breathe deeply before returning my gaze to his. "I'm pregnant."

Beckett freezes. His body stiffens, and he looks at me. The only movement is the unnatural ways his eyes are blinking. I give him a minute to process my words.

"You're pregnant?" he asks.

I nod.

"With my baby?"

"Of course."

"You're pregnant with my baby?"

I sigh. "Yes, Beckett. I am pregnant with your baby."

He releases my hands and leaps to his feet. Arms raised in the air, he howls, his face toward the ceiling as he jumps up and down on the sofa.

Startled, I spring off the sofa and stand beside it as I watch Beckett in what I can only assume is… celebration?

He bounces off the sofa. I flinch as he envelops me in an intense bear hug. He squeezes me tight, peppering kisses on the top of my head. Lifting me off the ground, he spins me in a circle, shouting, "I can't believe I'm going to be a dad!"

He sets me down but doesn't loosen his firm hug. "So you're happy about it?" I say into his chest.

He takes hold of my arms and pushes me back. Bending down, he looks at me at eye level. "Are you kidding with that question? Of course I'm happy. I'm more than happy. This is the best news I've heard all day, second to the part about you not divorcing me. Are you not happy about it?"

"Well, I wasn't thrilled when I thought about doing it all over again by myself."

"Elena." He shakes his head and pulls me into another embrace. "I love you so much, but the way in which you overthink things is going to be the death of me. If you thought for one second I wouldn't want to be in our child's life..." He doesn't finish his thought.

"I'm sorry, I was just in a bad place, and everything felt so dire and sad."

He tilts my chin up with his finger. "That's because you left me and hid from me and tried forcing us into a divorce that neither of us wanted. But now that all that is settled... you can see this for the blessing it is, right?"

New tears fill my eyes, these ones carrying the weight of overwhelming happiness and relief. "Yeah. I never thought I'd get to be a new mom again. I thought those years had passed. And I never imagined that I'd get to experience it all again with someone like you."

Beckett chuckles. "That's because, for some reason, you have it in your head that you're this decrepit old lady when the opposite is true. You're young, healthy, and by far the most gorgeous woman in any room you enter. Of course your body is capable of carrying life." He pauses, and his facial features soften as he holds me in a weightless gaze. "I'm so happy, Elena." The warmth of his voice fills my soul with hope. "When you told me you wouldn't be able to have more children, I admit, I was bummed. I've always wanted to be a dad, but I gave that dream up because I wanted you more. But a life with you and getting to be a parent alongside you is more than I could wish for. Thank you." He kisses my forehead.

"You never told me your dream was to be a dad."

"Of course not, and give you another reason to push me away?" He shakes his head. "I may be pretty, but I'm not dumb."

"Or humble," I tease.

"Agreed. Speaking of pretty. A kid with our genes... that child will be gorgeous!"

The smile that crosses my face is filled with genuine

joy. "Sure will."

"When's the baby due?"

I quickly calculate the due date in my head. "Not sure, exactly. But the baby should be born sometime in June."

Beckett's eyes go wide. "June? We're going to be playing in the Stanley Cup finals in June! What if the baby is born while I'm playing? I'll either have to miss the birth of my child or miss one of the games I've been working for my whole life."

"Calm down." I chuckle. "You're not even two months into the season. A lot can happen between now and then."

"Yeah, and that is qualifying for the Cup playoffs and kicking ass while in them. I'm telling you, babe. We're going all the way this season."

"Okay, well, even if that's the case," Beckett's eyes bug out, and I clarify, "which I have no doubt it is. The chances that I go into labor during one of your games is low. Don't worry. You'll be able to do both. See your child being born and winning the Stanley Cup."

He blows out a relieved breath. "You're absolutely right. Of course I will." He digs his hand in his pocket and kneels on the floor before me.

I bring my hands to my face in a gasp when I see the diamond in his hands. It's a 1920s-styled vintage ring. It has a platinum band with intricate filigree designs and a large round diamond in the center. If I had dreamed up the perfect diamond ring, it would've been this one. It's elegant, sophisticated, and glamorous. It's unique and feels like a one-of-a-kind, as if I'm the only woman in the world who will wear a ring this stunning, and in that way, it's reflective of our love —unlike any other and completely beautiful.

"Beckett..."

He holds the ring out to me, and I recognize it as one I saw in Vegas. It was in a jewelry store window across the aisle from the salon. Beckett wasn't with me when I saw it, so I have no idea how he knew.

"Elena, I want you to know that I love you more than anyone else in the world. When I married you in Vegas, in front of our friend Elvis with his weird puns and awful dance moves, I knew I'd never be single again from that day forward. We called it fake, but it never felt that way to me. You kept saying we had an end date, but I didn't believe that to be true. To me, you were always more. Always incredible. And from the moment I said, "I do," always mine. The connection we shared was special and intense from the very beginning. You are the person I've been waiting for my entire life. My love for you will never lessen. It is infinite. And the only way I can imagine loving you more than I do now is when I see you bring our child into this world. The mere thought of you holding the precious human we created blows my mind. I am so fortunate to have you, and I promise to spend the rest of my life making you feel like the most loved and cherished woman in the world because, in my world—you always will be. Elena, will you stay married to me?"

I release a half laugh, half sob of emotion and hold out my hand. "Yes, Beck. I will stay married to you."

He slides the ring onto my finger and pulls me down to him. He sits with his back against the sofa, and I straddle his legs. He snakes his hands up my back until his fingers claw through my hair, and he pulls my mouth to his. I release a satisfied sigh as his tongue dances with mine. God, I love this man.

I pull away. "You know, now that I've agreed to stay real married to you, there's no turning back. You're stuck with me. When I truly am an old lady, you'll have to take care of me."

He nods. "In five years' time when you're old, I will bring your cane and Ensure nutrient shake to you every morning."

I slap his chest and laugh. "Rude, Beckett."

He chuckles. "Seriously, I love you, and I always will."

"I love you." Our lips come together in a chaste kiss. "Is this ring from Vegas?"

"Sure is."

"How did you know?"

"Remember how I told you I went to the gift shop to get us those cheap bands to use for the ceremony? Well, I passed the salon and I saw you staring into the shop window. I waited for you to leave and I went to see what you were looking at. I bought it right then."

I hold out my hand and look at the beautiful ring. "Beckett, this was expensive. We were very much in the fake-wedding mindset then. Why would you waste money on a ring you may have never used?"

"I told you. My feelings for you were never fake. I think at the beginning they were confusing and maybe I didn't know exactly what they all meant, but I knew they were real. I knew that I was falling in love with you and that once we were married, I'd never want it to end. I also knew that I wanted you to have the ring that made you stop and stare with that expression of longing on your face."

Cupping his face, I press my lips to his. "How did I get so lucky? I've been waiting my entire life for you, Beckett Feldmore." Sitting on the hotel floor, I kiss Beckett with everything I have.

He breaks the kiss and pulls his phone from his pocket, moving his thumb across the screen.

I gasp, a wide smile forms on my face as the familiar song plays through the phone's speakers.

Beckett stands and extends his hand to mine.

"Dance with me."

I place my hand in his palm and he pulls me up from the floor and holds me against his chest as we sway to the music. Surrounded by the beautiful melody and enchanting lyrics of Elvis's, "Can't Help Falling in Love," Beckett kisses me just as he did in Vegas, after we said our vows.

The song that speaks to fools rushing in and falling madly in love because they can't help it fills my soul with happiness. It hits differently than it did in Vegas when I thought my feelings were an illusion of something more. It brought me sadness then. But now, there's only joy.

The song is perfect as is everything else. Our road here was wild, crazy, and so unlike me, but I know now that every minute of it was meant to be part of our journey. Nothing about Beckett and I should work, and yet, everything does.

Beckett kisses my neck. "You, Elena, are the dream I never knew to wish for. Thank you for coming true. You know what you being pregnant means?"

"What?"

"No more condoms. We can do it anywhere at any time."

I chuckle. "That's quite the transition, Beck. You go from dream coming true to barebacking it in a matter of two seconds."

"Well, they are two very important things." He presses his lips to mine. "We have a lot to do, you know? We have to find our dream house and move out of the condo. We'll have to get the nursery done. Oh, do you want a gender reveal party? Apparently, they're really popular. Annette in Accounting just had one. Do you want to get married again and have a bigger wedding or a reception with our friends?" He rattles off questions in rapid succession.

"Beckett." I press my lips to his to get him to stop talking. "My love. Those things can be figured out another day. Today, I just want to be with you."

"That's something I can get on board with. So tell me, is the bed in this joint as awful as this sofa?"

"No." I grin. "It's pretty nice."

"Good." He lifts me up, scooping me in his arms.

I wrap my arms around his neck and lean into his chest as he carries me to the bedroom. It's been a long week without my husband and I have no plans to leave this suite until we have to. It'll be just like our honeymoon. Orgasms and room service—I can't think of anything better.

My fingers play with the short hair at the nape of his neck. The ring that signifies a lifetime together feels heavy on my finger, a reminder that this is real.

This won't end.

This is forever.

# CHAPTER
## TWENTY-NINE

### BECKETT

This is a bye week unlike any other, and I can't say I hate it, and it's all courtesy of my wife. She found this stunning property in Texas, of all places. There were some initial grumbles, and admittedly, I was one of the ones complaining. In the past, our one week off in January, our bye week, has been spent at an exotic destination and in a luxury mansion. There's been a revolving door of women, tons of alcohol, lots of sex, and loads of fun.

Truthfully, except for the revolving door of women, all those things, at least for me, are still true. Elena came up with the idea to treat the entire Crane organization and their families to a luxury vacation, all expenses paid—also courtesy of my rich-ass wife.

Everyone came from the entire team and their loved ones to the accounting, PR, and human resources staff and their families. Remarkably, she even got my parents here.

She presented it as a weeklong celebration of our marriage since we never had a reception.

We've accomplished a lot in the last three months. My boys and I have maintained a winning season and are on target to make it to the playoffs. Elena and I bought a gorgeous house a few blocks from Cade and Iris and my parents, where we're going to raise our family.

Her father's mansion has been cleaned out and is being renovated. Elena is turning it into a home for pregnant and single moms to stay. The home will be stocked with food, toiletries, a room of professional attire that can be worn to interviews, a room full of children's clothing in all sizes, a computer lab with an instructor where several online courses, including one to help women earn their high school diploma, and lots of play areas for the kids that are fully staffed with childcare. The place she ran from in order to keep her child is now going to shelter those needing help to build a better life for theirs. It's a beautiful vision, and I'm so proud of her.

She's hired a handful of wonderful people to run the charities and businesses of Cortez Industries for her. She doesn't have plans to step down as the team doctor for the Cranes. She loves her job and wants to keep it. Selfishly, I'm glad. The only thing I love more than hockey is my wife, so getting to spend every day with both is a perfect life.

We decided not to redo the wedding. In all fairness, our Vegas one was perfect and something we'll always remember. So when she suggested turning bye week into a vacation celebrating us, I couldn't say no. Though I think it had less to do with us and was more an excuse to treat everyone we love to a special week.

This place has everything. The property has three mansions, one which is occupied by the players and is more lively. One is reserved for families with children. And the third is secretly called the old people's pad, which is reserved for everyone's parents. There are five pools, a golf course, a mini-golf course, a bumper car pad, a tennis and basketball court, and stables where we can ride horses. There's a huge kid's play area by the house where the families are staying that has every contraption a playground could have, including an area with a bunch of inflatable bouncy houses.

In the middle of it all is a common area, a huge patio with seating, tables, a fireplace, and a bar. It's covered by a roof held up by beams leaving the place open to the outdoors. Next to the patio is the largest pool on the estate. During the day, we all go there to grill out, play cards, and be together.

At night, the guys can retreat to the team's mansion and partake in any shenanigans they see fit.

"I'm calling it." Bash throws the remainder of his chips into the center of the table and smirks in Ariana's direction. "Alright, show us what you've got."

Ari smiles and lays out her hand. "Four kings! Beat that, Cookie!"

"Dammit." Bash throws his cards down. He grumbles, "Monster," under his breath.

Dreven sighs and tosses his hand onto the table as well.

"What about you, stepdad?" Ariana teases.

I slide my straight flush into a pile and place it face down on the table, my hand over the top of it. "You won it all. Congrats."

She raises her hands in the air and shrieks, celebrating the massive pot of money she won. Things between Ari and me have been great lately, and I don't want to rock the boat. As competitive as I am, I want Elena's daughter to like me more than I want to win a game of poker.

"Yeah, I'm heading in," Dreven states, pushing away from the table.

"Me too," I say.

I stand just as Bash reaches for my cards. "Let me see your cards."

Jerking my hand out, I mix the cards around with some others on the table. "I had a three-of-a-kind. Uh, nines."

"You're lying." He scoffs.

I shrug. "I guess we'll never know. Good game."

I find Elena sitting in a lounge chair, reading a book on her Kindle. She's wearing a lacy cover-up over her bathing suit. Votive candles on the table beside her give her skin a warm glow. She is absolutely beautiful. At three months pregnant, she really isn't showing yet. But just knowing that she's carrying our baby makes her hotter than ever. "You ready to go in?"

She looks up and smiles. "Do you want to drive around for a bit? Kiss under the full moon?"

My lips tug up at the sides. "Well, I'll never turn that down an invitation like that."

I extend a hand and pull her up.

A line of golf carts is parked past the main guest-house. The estate is big, so they've come in handy getting from place to place. We make our way to the one without a top. The owners of this place apologized, saying the last renters flipped the cart and broke its top off. They've ordered a replacement, but it's on back order, so they couldn't fix it before our stay. But the topless golf cart is our favorite. It allows us to stargaze on our rides at night.

"Do you want to drive?" I ask.

"Go for it." She steps into the passenger side of our convertible golf cart.

This place is huge with gorgeous scenery. On our drive last night, we saw a herd of deer and got pretty close to them before they ran off.

We drive along the pebblestone pathways for a while. The night is warm with a cool breeze. Elena scoots over to get closer to me.

"This is a good spot," she says.

I stop in front of a small cottage-styled home that is part of the property. We could've stayed here, but we wanted to be close to our family and friends, and this place is quite secluded, located a five-minute golf cart drive away from the larger mansions.

Elena threads her fingers through mine, and I hold her hand as she steps out of the cart and onto the grass. The bright full moon casts a glow onto everything.

"This place is really cute," she says as we walk around the blue cottage.

I step around a patch of wildflowers that have found a home along the path. "I guess it's for the guests that want more quaint lodging."

Behind the cottage is a pool, a fraction of the size of the others.

Elena tugs on my arm. "Let's go for a moonlit swim. Just the two of us."

I raise my eyebrows, my lips forming into a sly smile. "Well, that sounds very honeymoonish of us, doesn't it?"

Since Elena used this week as a reason to celebrate our marriage, we've jokingly considered many honeymoon activities, especially those I may not want to do right now. Like earlier when I was kicking ass in a game of one-on-one basketball with J-man, and she needed her feet rubbed. Honeymoon or not, I'd do anything she asked because she is my queen, and I love her beyond measure. Add in the fact that she's carrying my child, and it propels her to goddess level.

Standing to the side of the pool, I hold her hands between us as we tilt our heads back and look up at the dark sky full of stars and the bright moon.

"Only one more day," I say.

She sighs. "I know. I've had the best time. I love everyone here. I'm glad we were able to do this."

"Yeah, me too. You were right, it's been very special. I love that my parents are here and Ari. It's good for everyone to spend this time together."

"You know, next bye week, we're going to have a six- to seven-month-old." She squeezes my hands.

I chuckle. "I still can't believe it. I can't wait."

"Oh, you can wait." She holds back a laugh. "Come June, sleep will never be the same."

"It'll be worth it, though," I say.

"Yeah, it will."

We meet in the middle, our lips come together, and I revel in this kiss. I'm obsessed with kissing this woman. I lose track of time as we kiss, but suddenly, kissing her isn't enough. I need more. I have to touch her. With the way she rubs herself against my body, I know that she wants me, too. She needs it as much as I do, especially with all the pregnancy hormones racing through her body. Elena and I have always had amazing chemistry, but now, somehow, it's even better.

We are two of the same. Our wants are desperate, and our needs overpower all self-control while our lust screams the loudest.

I lift the bottom hem of her swim coverup. My hand slides underneath the fabric, finding its way to her bikini top. I run my finger under the curve of the wire. She moans into my mouth, pushing her pelvis into my leg, begging me to continue. I put my hand underneath the wire and push the fabric up until I can feel the weight of her softness in my hand. I run my thumb along the taut nipple before pulling and teasing it between my fingers. She squirms against me.

Our lips continue their assault on one another as my hand moves to the other side and repeats my movements. After I've paid equal attention to both of her breasts, my hand roams down her smooth belly to the elastic of her swim bottom. I run my fingers along the waistband, feeling the excited tremor of her skin.

I break our kiss and find her stare. Her eyes are hooded, her lips swollen, her hair tousled and sexy. God, my wife is gorgeous.

With one hand, I push down her bikini bottoms enough to grant me access. I slide my hand underneath the fabric, and she closes her eyes with a soft moan, her head falling back between her shoulder blades. I push two fingers into her entrance, taking pleasure in the warmth that wraps around me. I drop my head to her neck and breathe her delicate skin in as my hand moves. She grasps my arm and back, digging her fingers into my skin. Quiet whimpers come from her lips.

I drag my lips up and down her neck, kissing and sucking, unable to keep from tasting her. My fingers continue to savor her as the palm of my hand moves against her sensitive skin.

Writhing against me, she bites her lip, attempting to hold in her groans of pleasure.

"Oh God," she whispers into the night air. "Please, Beck, please."

I love the way my name falls from her lips, the way she begs me to touch her when that's all I want to do. It causes a storm of need to fill me up. My body threatens to blow with the sweet ache of all-consuming want. I've never wanted someone the way I want Elena. The intensity in which I need her is unlike anything I've felt.

"Beckett," she breathes. Her voice is so needy that she sounds like she's in pain.

"I got you." I kiss her neck as my hand picks up speed.

Her body quakes, and I kiss her lips, catching her cries in my mouth. My mouth continues to caress her lips until her body stops quivering. Then I move my kisses to her neck once more as she takes in breaths of air.

I take the kiss deeper. I kiss her hard, my tongue licking greedily. Her taste is addictive. She whimpers into my mouth as her fingers pull through my hair, drawing me closer.

She pulls her mouth from mine, her lips swollen and red, sexy. "You want to go skinny-dipping?"

"Absolutely."

"Me too." Her voice is low and seductive.

With just a few words, Elena has the ability to make me crazy with desire. She is exceptionally skilled at it.

I yank my T-shirt over my head and pull off my swim trunks while Elena removes her clothing.

The moonlight highlights her naked body. "You are a fucking goddess, and you're mine," I growl.

"I'm yours. Always." She leans in for a quick kiss before she leads us to the pool steps. The pool must be heated like the ones by the house because it's warm, even as the night air grows cooler.

Once in the water, I waste no time. Pressing my back against the side of the pool, I tightly hold Elena against me with one arm as my free hand slides down her wet skin and between her legs. Two of my fingers enter her.

She bites her lip at the intrusion, and a small moan comes from her lips, but she doesn't look away. Our lusty gazes stay connected.

"Does that feel good?" I ask as my fingers move deeper.

Elena closes her eyes and drops her face to my shoulder. "God, yes."

"Does that make you feel good, baby?" My thumb moves in circles around her most sensitive area.

"Yes," she whimpers quietly against my neck. Her fingers grab at the skin of my back.

I pull out my fingers and position my length at her entrance, and I push in. Every sensation of this experience is incredibly intense. The feeling of being out in the open and together in this way is hot as fuck. The warm water hitting my wet skin adds a different element and is highly enjoyable. And the way she feels without a barrier between us is incredible. Now that she's my wife, I never want to wear a condom again.

She continues to moan into my neck as my palms grasp her ass and push her onto me over and over again. I tilt my knees and bend my pelvis up, to make sure I'm hitting the exact spot she needs. I can tell by the forceful way in which her hands grasp my back with her jagged breaths against my skin and the almost painful-sounding moans that leave her mouth that she is so close. My arms burn as I continue to move her onto me, increasing my speed with each thrust as I chase my own release.

Finally, we're both there, and as her body shatters around me, I let go. I capture her cries in my mouth as I kiss her hard. Making love to my wife in this pool on this beautiful moonlit night is the single most satisfying moment in my life to date.

Until tomorrow, which will somehow be even better.

# CHAPTER
## THIRTY

ELENA

"You've got to be kidding me," I groan, the contractions coming harder now. Leaning over the desk in my office, my entire body tenses as a contraction takes over. My lips are in an O, and I breathe through the pain.

We've officially come full circle. Here we are in our home arena, the guys in the Cup finals, which is where I laid eyes on Beckett for the first time a little over a year ago. I watched Beckett cry out in pain as he was shoved into the boards, injuring his knee.

Now, I'm the one in pain, but this isn't round one of the playoffs. This is the final game, in the final round —*the* game Beckett has waited his entire life for.

The door handle turns, and I jolt upright. Beckett pops his head in. "Everything okay, baby?"

"Yes." I plaster on a smile. "I was just getting off my feet for a couple of minutes. Heading back out?"

He nods and smiles as if he's the happiest man in the world. "Yeah, this is it. This is it, babe."

I lift my arms, cradling his face in my hands. "I'm so proud of you. You deserve this. You have worked your entire life for this. Just go and do what you do. You got this. The Cup is yours."

He blows out a breath. "It's ours. We got this."

"You do."

"I love you so much." He kisses me.

"I love you. Now go get that cup."

Bending down, he kisses my belly, "for good luck" as he's been doing since my pregnancy belly popped out. He stands, kisses me again, and hurries out.

As soon as he's gone, I close the door and groan into my arm as another contraction hits.

This is not happening. The little cherub that's been happily bouncing on my bladder for months has refused to come out. Today marks ten days past my due date. My doctor has wanted to induce me for a couple of weeks now. Apparently, as a forty-one-year-old, I'm basically geriatric and considered high-risk in the pregnancy world. There hasn't been a time these past two weeks that would've been convenient, given the playoff schedule. We figured the baby was holding out until after tonight, when this would be over. But no, he or she was waiting until daddy was in the midst of his lifelong dream to join us.

I stand tall and rub my enormous belly. "Please give me this."

I realize begging my unborn child to wait a little longer is pointless, but I'm doing it anyway. My husband will not miss seeing his first child born. He will also not miss the last period of the Stanley Cup finals, and neither will I. I've grown to adore the Cranes organization and everyone here. The past year has been the best year of my life, and in part, I have these people to thank. They're my family now. I want to see our guys win the Cup as much as anyone. More importantly, I want to see Beckett's face when they do.

I pull out my phone and text Ari, who is sitting with the Feldmores and Iris, and ask her to meet me in the team's VIP box. The box is reserved for special guests of the coach and owners of the organization. But given it has glass that I can hide behind, it is where I will be.

Ari is standing outside the door to the VIP area when I get there. "Mom, are you okay? Are you in labor?"

"Yes," I answer, and her mouth falls open. "I have been all game, but the contractions are starting to get intense. So I need you to get word to Beckett that I'll be in the box for the last period. Do not tell him I'm in labor. Just say my feet are swollen, and I'm going to sit up here. It's a story he'll buy, considering how swollen my feet have been, and this VIP area has the most comfortable cushioned seats."

I bear down as another contraction hits. It consumes me with an intense wave of agony from my toes to my scalp.

"Mom. You need to go to the hospital. I'll go with you."

"No! I'm staying. I can make it another twenty minutes."

She huffs out a breath. "That's with no stops or overtime. You know we're currently tied with Vancouver, right?"

"I can do this. Labor takes hours and hours. Just please tell Beckett where I am. He'll worry when he doesn't see me, and I don't want it to affect his game."

"Okay, then I'm coming back up here and sitting with you, and if a baby's head pops out between your legs, I'm taking you in."

"Deal."

I barge into the VIP box and quickly relay the current situation before another contraction hits. Though with my sweat-glistened face and giant protruding belly, I think my predicament is pretty obvious.

Coach Albright's ex-wife stands from an oversized leather chair. "Here, take my seat. I'll grab one of the chairs over there."

"Thank you," I say, grateful for the comfortable place to sit. I heard the coach's ex-wife wasn't the nicest lady, but she got my stamp of approval.

The guys are getting in their positions. The period break is over. The referee stands in the center of the ice, ready to drop the puck. Bash stands in the face-off spot, waiting for the puck to fall. Beckett looks up at the box, and his face breaks into a smile when he sees me. I plaster a grin on my face, give him a thumbs-up, and blow him a kiss.

My heart melts at the sight of him, and I beam with pride. I love my husband so much. I truly don't like to think about how it felt to live a life without him because it feels as if he were always meant to be mine. Two minutes into the game, Ari joins me in the box. I do a double take when I notice Bash's jersey number across her chest. "Why are you wearing Bash's jersey?"

She looks down at her attire as if she had forgotten what she was wearing. "Oh, I didn't really even think about the number. I forgot all my Cranes clothing in my apartment, so I picked one up in the store downstairs before the game started. I just grabbed the first jersey in my size."

"Oh, okay," I say before another contraction consumes me. Ari grabs a pillow from the sofa in the back of the suite and stands in front of me, blocking me from view, as I scream into it. I don't know why yelling like a madwoman helps the pain, but it does. I don't spare a glance to my side to see what I'm sure are looks of abject terror on the faces of my suite mates because every second that I'm not consumed with pain has to be spent watching the game.

"If you go to the hospital, you can get an epidural to help with the pain, Mom. Beckett will understand."

"No," I cry. I want to see him win this. I wave my hand through the air. "And it doesn't matter anyway. I'm quite positive I'm past the epidural stage. I'm sure I'm too dilated. Looks like I'm doing this the all-natural way."

Having this baby without modern medicine to reduce the discomfort wasn't part of my birth plan, but I'm not surprised it's going this way. This is Beckett's child, after all, and it is going to do exactly what it wants.

Three minutes left in the game and we're still tied, two to two. It's been a stressful back-and-forth game with both opponents equally matched with talented players.

"If this goes into overtime, I may die." The words leave my mouth before I think about their ramifications. The utter horror on Ari's face causes me to chuckle. "It's a joke, my love."

She rolls her eyes. "Not a funny one, Ma."

Two minutes left.

"Come on!" Ari and I cheer in unison.

One minute left.

"Please sweet baby Jesus. Come on, baby!"

Tears stream down my face, and a cluster of emotions swell within. I'm so proud and anxious and worried and hopeful and in agony all at once. My heart beats rapidly in my chest as I pray for a win for the Cranes. "Come on. Come on."

I cry and scream through the contractions openly now, the sound muffled by the roar of the crowd. Every fan in the arena proudly displaying their navy and white Cranes attire has been dreaming of this moment for years. It's been decades since this organization has won the cup.

Thirty seconds left.

The Cranes have possession. Cade races down the ice, a Vancouver player by his side. Bash breaks free of his defender and rushes the man on Cade, slowing him down just enough to give Cade an opening. His stick smacks the puck, and it slices in the air toward Beckett, who has a defender blocking him. Beckett turns toward the boards, and faster than I've seen him skate, he spins around his defender. Shards of ice fly around him as he circles the Vancouver player until he's between him and the puck.

Beckett stops the moving puck with his stick and, without a moment's hesitation, slaps the puck toward the Vancouver goal. Halko, the goalie, lunges toward the corner of the net, his gloves missing the puck as it whips by and hits the back of the net.

The buzzer sounds, and the stadium explodes.

Ari and I jump up and down, hugging one another as tears fall. The roar of the crowd is so loud the stadium vibrates. The Cranes rush on the ice and fall over one another in a giant huddle of celebration. Sobs wrack my body as overwhelming joy fills me up. I can't even imagine what Beckett is feeling at this moment.

"Are you okay?" Ari asks, concern lining her features.

I continue to jump, crying hysterically and holding my belly. "Never better!"

She smiles and celebrates with me.

Beckett looks up at the box and holds his arm up with his pointer finger in the air, looking like the happiest man in the world. I hold up my pointer finger, and with a huge smile on my face, I yell, "Number one, baby!"

The giant silver cup is brought out onto the ice and handed to Beckett. He raises it over his head and roars, skating in a circle, hyping the fans up.

I've never been in a place with this many happy people, and the energy is out of this world. I hope someone is taking lots of pictures of my man holding that cup over his head because this is a moment I want to remember for the rest of my life. Not that I could ever forget it.

Another contraction hits, and this time the pressure is so strong it feels like my butt is going to explode. I remember that sensation from Ari's delivery, and her arrival came shortly after.

I grab her arm as I double over in pain. "We gotta go. Come on."

As we hurry to my car, I call Iris and tell her to get Beckett to the hospital as fast as possible. I couldn't risk sending Ari through the excited crowd to tell him. It might take too long. This baby is coming soon, and as much as I love this place and the people in it, I'm not having my baby here.

The pressure grows as Ari races toward the hospital, and I'm starting to wonder if I waited too long to leave. The front seat of a car isn't high on my delivery location list either.

She swerves into the emergency room circle drive.

A hospital employee in scrubs comes out to meet us. Ari jumps out of the car.

"She's having a baby like right now."

In a matter of seconds, I'm in a wheelchair being pushed to the labor and delivery unit. The louder I am through my contractions, the faster the employee pushes me.

A nurse helps me into a gown, and then I'm on the hospital bed. The on-call doctor comes in and does a quick check. "You're fully dilated, fully effaced, and I feel the head. It's time to push," she says.

"No. I can't. Not without my husband. We have to wait."

"We can wait a few minutes, maybe, but that baby is coming whether we're ready or not."

Ari holds my hand as I scream through a few more contractions. Sweat drips down my face, mixing with my tears. I need Beckett.

"You have to start pushing. The baby is ready," the doctor says.

"No! I can't. Not without my husband." I look at Ari and sob. "I need Beckett."

"I'm here!" Beckett sprints into the room. His hair is still wet with sweat, and it's clear he changed out of his pads and uniform at record speed. He wears a random pair of sweatpants and a T-shirt as he races toward me. "I'm here, baby."

"Oh, thank God," I cry as another contraction hits, and this time, I push.

Beckett holds my hand and rubs my sweat-soaked hair away from my face as I push through every contraction. It's complete agony, and I hate every second of it, but fifteen minutes later, a slimy, warm, sweet little boy is being placed against my chest.

Tears roll down Beckett's face. "It's a boy!"

"It's a boy," I cry, kissing my baby's head.

Beckett sits beside me on the sofa in our living room as we stare at the baby in my arms, one of our favorite pastimes. Nolan Cole Feldmore came into this world exactly when he wanted. He's a week old, and I already know he's going to take after his father—beautiful, bold, and fearless.

We chose not to find out the gender of the baby before he was born, and the surprise was so special. I'll never forget the look on Beckett's face when he realized he was a father to a little boy. I'm sure he has a hundred different toddler hockey setups in his Amazon cart, ready for purchase.

We chose the name Nolan because it means champion and Cole because it means victorious, both Beckett's ideas, but I liked the sound of them. Poor kid has a lot to live up to now that his dad scored the winning goal for the Cranes Stanley Cup Victory.

My past life of struggle, save for the wonderful memories I made with Ari, barely hold residence in my mind anymore. It's hard to recall who I was before when who I am now is everything I've ever wanted to be—a mom, a doctor, surprisingly enough a wife, and most of all—happy.

This baby will live a life surrounded by love. Our family and friends are some of the most incredible people. Ari is staying with us for a couple of weeks, making sure I have everything I need. I love that she has this extended family, too. For years, it was the pair of us against the world, and it worked. She was happy and loved. But now she is adored by so many more, and she deserves all the love in the world.

Beckett's mother and Iris have stopped by to deliver meals every day and of course to hold little Nolan. All the Cranes have visited and are still on a high from the cup win followed by the arrival of Nolan on the same night. It will be a day we'll all remember forever.

It's hard to compare my past life to my current one. I feel as if I was a different person then. One's circumstances change who they have to be. My world was tightly controlled because it had to be for my survival.

I was always a couple of bouts of bad luck away from losing everything.

In my new era, a massive weight has been lifted off me, and I can be free. Part of that is circumstance. But the realization that life could be this way was a hundred percent Beckett-driven. He taught me to let go and breathe. He showed me how it feels to be loved unconditionally. He gave me this little life in my arms. He's supported me through all my endeavors over the past year, never allowing me to believe that there was anything I couldn't do.

Nothing about Beckett's love isn't real, raw, and true.

He loved me enough to allow me to let go.

I'm no longer afraid, just blissfully happy.

It's simple, really. The answer to so many things is love.

Beckett was always meant to be mine. I just had to wait for him to find me.

Now that he has, I'll never let him go.

Dear Readers,

If you're reading this, thank you! Without you, I wouldn't be able to have my dream job. I hope you loved reading Beckett and Elena's journey as much as I loved writing it. This was my first time writing a fake marriage, reverse age gap story and it was so fun! I'm having a blast writing hockey romance, which in true Ellie Wade style is just an emotionally charged love story with a side of hockey lol. So hopefully whether you're a sports romance reader, a lover of my emotional reads, or a fan of the fake marriage trope, you loved this one.

I'm planning on Crane Hockey being a four book series. But of course, if enough readers request, I can always write more. Next up is Gunner's book, One Pucking Wish! It is going to be an enemies to lovers, forced proximity, one bed trope. \*\*claps hands\*\* It will be releasing in five short weeks and you're going to love it!

In case you missed it, I wrote a 5,000 word bonus holiday epilogue for Elena and Beckett. Check the link in my bio on any of my social media accounts for the link to the bonus epilogue.

I've said this many times, but this is a hard job. In truth, it's the most difficult job I've ever had yet I love it so much. I love writing love stories with flawed characters that have to work for their HEA. Thank you for reading so I can continue to write.

Thank you for every social media post share or comment, every message, review, or recommendation to your book friends. It all matters, and it all gives authors the fuel to keep going in a very brutal industry. I truly can't express just how grateful I am to every single one of you.

Make your life a beautiful one.

Forever,

Ellie <3

# OTHER TITLES BY ELLIE WADE

For information on Ellie's books, please visit her website.

www.elliewade.com

## The Choices Series

A Beautiful Kind of Love

A Forever Kind of Love

A Grateful Kind of Love

## The Flawed Heart Series

Finding London

Keeping London

Loving London

Eternally London

Taming Georgia

## The Beautiful Souls Collection

Bared Souls

Kindred Souls

Captivated Souls

Fated Souls

Destined Souls

Entwined Souls

**The Crane Hockey Series**

One Pucking Love

One Pucking Heart

One Pucking Wish

One Pucking Destiny

**The Heroes of Fire Station Twelve**

Fragment

Found

Fated

**Standalones**

Forever Baby

Chasing Memories

A Hundred Ways to Love

**Cherry Blossom Grove**

*Ellie Wade's Sweet Collection*

Licorice Wishes

**Boxed Sets**

The Flawed Heart Series

The Choices Series

The Beauty in the Journey Collection

Crane Hockey

# ABOUT THE AUTHOR

Ellie Wade resides in southeast Michigan with her husband three children, and three dogs. She loves the beauty of her home state, especially the lakes and the gorgeous autumn weather. When she is not writing, you will find her reading, snuggled up with her kiddos, or spending time with family and friends. She loves traveling and exploring new places with her family.

Made in the USA
Monee, IL
04 December 2023

48202836R00184